This Indigo Is Violet Eve

by

Katherine Highland

© Katherine Highland 2024
Cover design and images © Katherine Highland 2024

You may quote or reproduce content, but the source should be acknowledged.

If quoting from any sources linked to in this book, please seek the relevant permissions from those sources.

This novella explores an autistic woman's experience of bereavement, both practically and emotionally, in detail. Sources of help, guidance and support, including those mentioned within the story, are UK or Scotland specific and can be found in the sections at the end of the book. The story also contains some swearing and discussion of sensitive subjects. It is an own voices work written to promote understanding as well as to entertain; expect a high proportion of divergent, particularly autistic and aspec (on the aromantic and / or asexual spectrum), characters and exploration of issues interwoven with the storyline. It also contains some mild spoilers for the Inverbrudock trilogy.

ISBN: 9798324715069

Profits from the sale of this book in printed and electronic form go to Autism Initiatives (Scotland) to support their one stop shops for autistic adults.

1

A Convivial Evening

"He's from Denmark and he's never seen the Northern Lights?!"

Diane Abercrombie's jaw dropped at this revelation about her close friend Bethany Sawyer's new boss.

"Well, he's always lived in cities; Odense until he was a teenager, then his family moved to Glasgow, which is actually slightly further north in latitude."

"True enough. I always think of the culturally Scandinavian countries as being further north than us, and of course the light pollution in cities is a factor"; Diane brushed pale strands of blonde hair back from her face as a thoughtful expression entered her grey eyes. "It's a bit of a conflict of interest for me with my love of seeing the streetlights on! I thought I'd be sure to have seen the aurora by now, since I moved to Arbroath and then here to Inverbrudock where there are beaches, but I'm so often in bed with my devices switched off for the night when alerts come through on the app. I'm often too tired to get changed again and go out if I am up when they come through, and I've had so many disappointments when I have made myself go out. My phone has picked up a slight glow that may or may not have been, but there's never been a definitive display that I could be sure of what I'd seen. I know that what our eyes pick up is often a lot fainter than the spectacular photos you see especially in this country, but I would have thought I'd have seen something more identifiable by now. Well, maybe now Magnus has moved to Perth, he'll have his best odds yet!"

"I hope so; he deserves it"; Bethany picked at a thread on her light green linen overshirt, idly wondering whether it was annoying her enough to make it worth getting the mini scissors out of her bag. Diane wouldn't mind; she would understand the pressing need to deal with the distraction. "My luck certainly turned when Nadine moved on and he took over as manager. He's so kind and laid back. The other day, Tommy was sorting a delivery and a current social policy book got in with the stock for the fiction shelves by accident. It was a genuine mistake; the author's name was similar to one of our best-selling fiction writers. Magnus pointed it out to him, but privately, and he thought it was hilarious. He and Tommy had a laugh about it and moved on. No harm done and no lecturing. Nadine would have hit the roof about it potentially being taken as a prank to make a political statement and drawing the company into controversy."

"Sally would have seen the funny side of that too. She and I often pick up on things that other colleagues either don't notice or don't find funny enough to provoke a reaction. Last week I was in for my supervision with her; we had a cup of tea afterwards and Colin who does the stationery orders popped his head around the door to say that there was an ongoing shortage of envelopes but the supplier was addressing it. Well, Sally and I looked at each other and..."; Diane mimicked their faces crumpling with mirth. "Colin realised the joke; he joined in with the laughter but a couple of the other project workers were in the room and they gave the three of us that puzzled look; you know the one. As in when we don't get their humour it's us being slow or joyless, but when they don't get something we find funny, it's us being weird. The best one, though, was when we were in negotiations with the local council about a possible new scheme and we were told in no uncertain terms that we were to call it 'a proof of concept', not 'a pilot'. The Chairman was due to visit and give a talk about it; we were all gathered in the main meeting room and then Verena came in to tell us she'd had a message that he had been delayed due to an emergency with his heating system at home. To be fair, this was back when we had that unseasonable cold spell and his elderly mother lives with him. Anyway, I said 'Can he not get the proof of concept light to come back on?' Sally was bent over laughing. Verena was her usual stoic, professional self but had a sudden pressing need to check something in her briefcase; we both saw her shoulders shaking."

"No wonder! You seem to have a better working relationship with Verena these days though?"

"Yes, I'd say so; there will never be the warmth and trust there that I have with Sally, but do you know what; I'm fine with it. Civil and surface-level cordial is all I look for from her. Sally is the important one, being my supervisor, and I feel as safe with her as I ever could in a workplace. A supportive line manager makes all the difference. You seem much more relaxed too since Magnus took over from Nadine."

"I am; now that I'm getting used to having that safety again, I'm realising how much I'd lost when Anita left and I found myself back at square one with Nadine. When Magnus had his one to one introductory chats with all of us, he asked about anything we would like to see done differently or directions we'd like to see the bookshop take, in terms of inclusion, community etc. As you can no doubt imagine, that set me off. I said I wish we would do more to promote minority authors; all well and good and valid. But then I kicked off about all the success and big money going to already privileged authors and their causes; good ones, but already well supported. I had to go and use Morton Pargeter as an example, didn't I. Rich white American who supports a couple of well known international charities out of his profits and everyone knows about it because he's so well established by a system that favours people like him. I did clarify that it wasn't a criticism of *him*, but that it's frustrating when own voices independent authors struggle to get seen at all. Of course, I had to think fast because it nearly backfired on me. Not only is he one of Magnus' favourite authors, but he met him at a signing in Copenhagen when he was a boy; part of a tour close to Morton Pargeter's heart, because he's of Scandinavian descent. The name Morton as used in his maternal great-grandfather's family would originally have been Morten. You'd think my interest in the etymology of names would have flagged that up as a possibility and made me think before I blundered; that I might be insulting my new boss's heritage, as well as having no way of knowing what he thought of him as an author! I was horrified and in the past I would have fled, but I somehow kept calm and apologised, and Magnus didn't hate me for my clumsy faux pas. He apologised for having made me feel as though I'd said the wrong thing; said he was impressed at my principled answer and his enjoyment of Morton Pargeter's writing took nothing away from the truth of what I had said. He told me it had given him valuable insight into an aspect of what we as a business can do that he may not otherwise have thought of. He owned his own privilege in not having had to think about it that way. It was such a relief especially given my hopes of him being receptive to our idea of incorporating your autistic hygge concept into a sensory reading room. Which he was, and he's excited to meet up with us about it."

"You handled that amazingly; well done! I know how much it will have bothered you, but I'm proud of you and I'm definitely seeing the change in you since you started letting other people in more; letting go of that need to do everything on your own. And it's not clumsiness, especially when it comes from that place of passion about justice for overlooked people. It's trauma and damage from all the years of having to work so much harder to be accepted; to be forgiven for mistakes, to have room to go through learning experiences without being written off in the name of 'safeguarding' or being 'a liability' due to 'bewareness' of our neurotype. The fact that something you said, which is perfectly valid, felt as though it didn't fit the audience because of his own personal taste in reading and a memory from his early life which there was no reason for an employee to know about is not a blunder. Nobody can know all the variables in their audience. It's seen through a lens of 'autistic people are socially clumsy and have no sense of nuance or empathy', which is why we don't get away with it as others do and that is discrimination. Seeing an entirely natural part of social interaction differently because the person speaking is autistic is society's failing, not yours. The fact your inner voice is telling you that you somehow should have seen a potential conflict because an author's name has possible Scandinavian origins and your boss is Danish is a classic example of how much our fears around getting things wrong can get out of hand. Hindsight is seen as accurate but it can be hypervigilant too. It's logical to want to get off to a good start with a new boss, but it's our learned 'fawn' response to the ingrained patterns of rejection, linked to the fight, flight or freeze instincts, that makes us feel we can only do so by having identical views. You need to focus on how positively Magnus reacted and that you made him think; you challenged the established hierarchy of privilege and got a result."

"True. I did sound judgemental when I talked about Morton Pargeter though; I would have adjusted my tone had I known, or thought to account for the possibility, of Magnus being a fan. It was wrong of me regardless because Morton Pargeter isn't the problem; the system is. Fortunately, Magnus is keenly on our wavelength. He gets how a sensory reading room would be of benefit, or at least enjoyment, to non-neurodivergent people too and how effective that can be for breaking down barriers. Yes, there will be people who will have concerns about appropriation or watering down autistic spaces, but it's possible to combine the two aims; for instance, have times - more than an hour here and there - when the space is for autistic people only."

"Well, yes; after all, hygge is from Danish culture so it's already being appropriated and I'm glad Magnus is OK with that! It's so positive though; it's applying it in ways which will help others while staying true to and acknowledging its roots."

"Indeed. It's going to be good for me to get into the way of sharing the process with a team on something which wasn't my idea or all my own work. Part of managing my fatigue has to be learning to let myself collaborate; to feel that I'm enough and having a part in something bigger rather than having to do it all alone in order to earn credit is enough for me to have a place in the world and to deserve support to stay well. Working on this with people who have demonstrated I can trust them, like you and Magnus, is going to be ideal for developing that; for learning to let go of the need to be solely in control, while maintaining my own autonomy and covering my own back; keeping records and copies of everything. Not because I think I'll need to with you two, but because it's the right thing for anyone collaborating on a creative project to do; it's the precedent I want to set. Not to mention mollifying the 'Now Be Careful, naïve little autistic with no understanding of the big bad world' brigade!"

"Indeed; we cannot drop our guard with them! Always waiting to pounce and hold it against us forever or close off opportunities to us if the smallest precaution slips through the net or anything goes wrong which they can pin on our ineptitude! And they're always 'Just Saying'. What does that even mean? We saw their lips move and heard the pre-emptivomit spew out."

"Pre-emptiwhatnow?"

"Ah! Jocelyn, one of the advisers at Up For Work; one of those clucky types"; Diane grimaced as she recalled the conversation with a colleague who had a tendency to service-user her despite Diane not being in a client situation with her. "She Had Concerns; not about you, but Magnus being a boss and new to both of us, that my ideas may be absorbed into something corporate and taken above both of our innocent little heads. I've told her before, I'm more than aware that I can't get paid for my input outside of my permitted work arrangement, other than expenses, without it affecting my benefits. I'm perfectly clued in that disabled people should not have to give our time and skill for free and see already salaried people take the rewards. But the way I see it, why should I keep positive input to myself because the system is unfair? Unlike many people, I am not being left short. I am privileged enough to have had the support to make successful applications for benefits; which are my equivalent of a living wage. And I can, although not within the parameters of what would be asked of a paid employee, give something back. Therefore I am contributing to society and the benefit system which allows me to do so at the level I can manage is paying me to do so. Those who can't shouldn't have to; those who can should be able to without it destabilising our income. The system is far from perfect. Yes, maybe I ought to be able to get something extra for putting in work on a creative project. But not getting anything over and above what I already get in benefits is not, for me in my personal circumstances, enough reason not to do something when I am able. Yes, I am conscious of my responsibility not to set a precedent for other disabled people to be expected to give their time and lived expertise for free. That's why I am talking about this with my line management; since my volunteering became permitted work and we're a company that liaises with employers about helping disabled people into work when it is suitable for them, it makes sense to share it with them and potentially make the project stronger. I'm covering myself by keeping them in the loop to make it more likely I can incorporate it into the working arrangements I already have. Jocelyn did eventually acknowledge that I'm switched on enough to have thought of all this. So I asked her, why did she feel the need to rain on my parade?, and that didn't feel strong or bespoke enough; I've already had it up to here with this sort of thing from a particular friend in the past and it took some working through as you know. I don't have the energy to go through all that again with another person I have to see regularly constantly thinking the worst of my judgement. So I said, 'never mind rain on it; pre-emptivomit all over it!' Oh, she was 'Just Saying'. Urgh! Of course, It's Just Because She Cares! Guilt dumped squarely back on my shoulders; the Jekyll and Hyde switch of dominant superior sage to poor unappreciated misunderstood victim."

"Oh, I feel that. The 'Just Saying' and 'Because I Care' manipulation is endemic."

"It is. I probably shouldn't have told Jocelyn anything about our plans, but it was one of those conversations where I was already having a tired day and I didn't have the energy to divert the topic or lie. I wish she could see how much it raises the stakes, the pressure on me as a neurodivergent, trying to be constructive in such a risk-averse system while she and her ilk can 'be human' without it bringing down their entire credibility."

"Well, I've got the list of autistic hygge ideas we've talked about; bookmarks with stimmable charms on the bit that hangs outside the book, blankets with a choice of coloured and textured patches people can attach with press studs, tinted overlays to put over the pages, a favourite quotes jar for people to write down and share what gave them glimmers and glows."

"Yes; I think you've covered everything there. I'm so glad that Magnus is on board with this, and supportive of you in general. You deserve it. I know Nadine tried in her own way but she never truly got it, did she? Sally is so up for the journey with me, and even Verena is gradually losing the 'here be monsters' fear she had around me. I know now, with detachment and hindsight, that it was definitely an alterous attraction of some sort I had there; not what people thought it was, and she seems to have forgiven me. Probably because now, all I'm bothered about where she's concerned is that I feel welcome when I have to go into the office for work reasons. So I guess I'll be giving out a different vibe; one that doesn't make her so squeamish."

"All the same, there's nothing to forgive regardless of if it had been a romantic or sexual attraction. You didn't do anything to her! People need to stop desexualising us and being offended by the very idea of our private thoughts being anything other than pure and innocent! Respecting that neurodivergent and disabled people can be aspec and know our own minds about it and that it counts, and refusing to entertain the idea that any of us can be sexual at all, are two extremely different things!"

"Indeed. I'm so glad that we both have better work lives now! I wished that I could transplant some of Sally's supportive attitude into Nadine when you were set back so much by her."

"Yes; here's to those days being behind us. I'm so looking forward to our teamwork on this. As well as it being better for my energy levels, I've come to understand that projects that succeed do involve collaboration; if there's a figurehead who gets all the credit, they don't often do all the gruntwork. Or if they do, they have the load taken off them in other ways in order to meet their needs and allow them the energy and headspace to focus. I'm not referring to people who take credit for other people's efforts here; that's a different problem. Whoever is the face of any project may well have genuinely put a lot of work in, but they won't have done it in isolation. I've been aspiring to what it looks like from the outside, not how it really is; believing that was how it had to be if whatever I did were to be enough. Life is beginning to feel much more settled and hopeful"; Bethany shivered suddenly as an unexpected draught found the back of her neck, incongruous in the warm room and the early August humidity. Farolita, Diane's blue point Siamese cat, lifted her head in the plush warm mocha nest of her bed in the corner; velvet dusky grey ears pricked up as she opened ice-blue eyes and rasped out a rusty awoken miaow.

"I'm sorry, did we disturb you?"; Diane laughed as she glanced fondly over at her pet. "Well, since my cat would seem to have called last orders, shall we have another glass of wine before your train?"

"Sounds like a plan!"; Bethany smiled broadly as she handed over her almost empty glass. Farolita stood up in her bed, arched her back and extended her front paws across the light ecru carpet in a classic long feline stretch before sashaying over to jump into Bethany's lap. She stroked the beautiful cat, who purred and padded blissfully, letting out a commanding yowl as Diane returned with the full glasses.

"Oh, it's like that, is it? This is her latest thing when I have company; she likes to lie across two laps. Des and I always sit together anyway with Jason opposite so that he can lipread, so it's gotten her into the habit." She handed Bethany her drink and sat down next to her on the broad, terracotta orange two-seater couch, leaving its identical opposite number where she had been sitting before empty.

"I get how that's easier for Jason, but how do you feel about it with your dislike of physical contact?"

"Honestly, I've found that I like, especially with someone in my immediate circle like you, Des or Sharon, to sit closely side by side. I think it's because it's less enclosed and there isn't the whole 'which side to put my face towards' dilemma; I think that's a lot of what puts me off hugging. I'm still not a hugs person, but I do like a bit of physical contact and it can feel lonely; I wish I could be comfortable with hugs. I always felt I was weird because I'd find it comforting to be sat close to a stranger on a busy train when I had much less social contact than I do now, yet I never wanted to hug the few friends I had when I saw them. I also felt that I was perpetuating the stereotype of autistic people being aloof, emotionless and standoffish! So it's been a revelation finding out what sort of contact works for me."

"Well, that's positive, and you don't need me to tell you that you don't owe anyone an explanation of not liking hugs or of any other boundary you have. It's good that you've discovered something that genuinely works for you, but touch aversion isn't a flaw or a negative to be cured or found a way around to accommodate people. Yes, I do like hugs, though I would never want or enjoy anyone hugging me out of any sense of 'should' when they're not comfortable. And your bodily autonomy has nothing to do with defining how deeply you feel nor how benevolent you are as a person! I've often backed off from a hug or kiss on the cheek, not because I was averse to it but purely because I didn't realise that was what the person was going to do, then had them act all wounded and martyred. I've learned it's marginally easier to let them think I'm lacking in personality than to spout some excruciatingly awkward explanation."

"Which, as you said, they're not owed anyway!"

"Touché! How are Des and Jason doing?"

"They're grand. They were in London visiting family for a couple of weeks last month. You've seen the photos of Luke enjoying his holiday here with his mum"; Diane stroked the half of her cat which was currently occupying her lap, ears twitching at the mention of her son's name. "Their trains never seem to get delayed either. I said to Des the other day, 'You two are so lucky, if you found an Oyster card holder in the street down there, it would have a pearl in it'!"

"Good one! Stacey at my work is like that; gets picked for everything, arrangements always go smoothly for her. Or at least it seems that way, compared to my haplessness and given how acutely observant she is about it"; Bethany rolled her eyes. "For instance, a couple of weeks ago an angry customer came in complaining about not having received a pre-order. We had three copies of the book in stock by then, so Magnus had cleared me to take one from the shelf to fulfil the order. I went to get it, just after another customer had grabbed all three copies for herself and two friends whose birthdays were coming up, as she'd told Stacey at the till. I was freaking out because I couldn't find it; looking around to see if it had been misfiled, checking the place on the shelf which corresponded to the author's first name initial as opposed to the surname, then I bolted into the office to tell Magnus and he came with me to speak to the customer and obviously after they had gone, Stacey told us about having sold the copies. 'Only you could be so unlucky, Bethany', she said. Mind you, Magnus wasn't having that. 'That's not the kindest thing you could say to your colleague, especially when she was using her initiative and trying her best to help a customer with something that wasn't her fault, Stacey'. You should have seen her face. And really it was the poor customer who was unlucky, but I was the one who got to look like a loser."

"Or she was the one who looked incredibly crass, cruel and immature! Magnus was right to call it out; I know it's harder for you to feel that vindication. You don't see how gracious it shows you to be that you recognise that your customer was the one who got a bum deal, and you feel for them despite being on the receiving end of their frustration about something that wasn't your job. It's easier to internalise Stacey's hot air because it aligns with how you reflexively feel about yourself, for all you have more insight and balance as time goes on."

"I know, and I am truly thankful for being in a better place in myself and with better people in the picture now. It's just not going to change me overnight."

"Oh, I get that; I'm not criticising you at all. I'd be a hypocrite if I were. I know how hard it is to take the small wins and build something from them as the gale of same old same old keeps on blowing it down."

"That's exactly how it feels. So I guess I need to keep weathering the storm; it's true what they say about the darkest hour being just before the dawn. I do believe the light is getting closer, and this project is a big part of it. I will keep on focusing on that. So, Des and Jason; they had a good time in London?"

"They did. They especially enjoyed catching up with their cousin Ronnie; in fact that was a bit of an adventure because the three of them went to visit their Aunt Shirley in Baronet Heights and her mega socialite neighbour had locked herself out. Ronnie offered to jimmy the window for her and let her in the door then make sure it was all secure afterwards; he's so considerate. She'd given them all the pursed mouth, racist side-eye and said 'This isn't the sort of community where we propose actions like that. Jimmy the window indeed!', and Ronnie said, 'Oh, I beg your pardon; would you like me to *James* the window?' I gather a prohibitively expensive out of hours locksmith was called in the end. Each to their own!"

Bethany howled with laughter. "James the window! I love it! I can picture Des and Jason telling that story too. I bet it's not much fun for Shirley though, with a neighbour like that. When will you next be getting together with the lads?"

"Next weekend; I'm helping them out in the café as three of the volunteers are on holiday"; Diane and Bethany both smiled at the mention of 'Harriet's Haven', the brothers' business which had resurrected the ahead of its time neurodivergent-friendly ethos of a long gone earlier establishment in the same building. Diane had been instrumental in bringing together the people, resources and ideas needed to reinstate Joan Morley's dream of a sanctuary whose pace and principles welcomed all. It had particularly resonated with the needs of people like the aunt Joan never knew; a child who died in a tragic road accident as a direct result of a vital therapeutic space being brutally taken from her.

"Jocelyn said that Des and Jason sounded to her like Godfrey and Jeremy when I explained that they're brothers. You know, from 'Trials'; that sitcom with the stuffy lawyers, their down to earth grandfather and their staff with the hectic love lives. Where to start with that? Besides the obvious, that is; there are few stronger examples of white privilege in sitcoms than that pair."

"Oh, good grief. And who would that make you then; Roxy the secretary?"

"Hardly. I doubt even Jocelyn would see any parallel there."

"She accepts you're aromantic and asexual, then?"

"It's not so much my being aroace; she knows I could never do a job with that degree of emphasis on taking phone calls!"

A clock chimed from the High Street, its sonorous toll buffed smooth by the salt in the coastal air as it called time through the invisibly shifting sands of the muggy summer twilight. Bethany drained her glass; the cat stirred and slid from her lap as she made herself cross that steep bridge between warm inertia and the jagged whirl of getting home.

Late evening air flowed cooler than before; more merciful to the clash of fabric on chafed skin, more sympathetic to the wrung-out huddle of every strand of hair. A patchwork of solidarity, amusement and optimism draped itself around Bethany's hazily relaxed shoulders as she walked and sat and walked again; familiarity spinning its tenuous web from muscle memory to well-trodden paths of routine. She turned the key in her front door; messaged Diane to confirm her safe arrival; got on with the usual coming in activities.

Without precedent at this hour, her land line telephone rang.

2

The Telephone Call

Brutally unexpected yet having lurked somewhere in the future ever since Bethany was a child, the phone call bombed into the most unremarkable of moments. She was halfway between her bathroom and the compact kitchenette of her Perth flat, having finished drying her hands, on her way to get a glass of water. Her mind, gently relaxed, must have been pleasantly replaying a snippet of conversation from her optimistic, morale-boosting evening with her best friend; she would never recall precisely which memory had been making her smile as the shock of the telephone ringing crashed into the quiet air.

The sensory jangle of an unplanned phone call always painfully jarred Bethany's ears, but this particular instance held an extra fullness of sound; a brimming of portent which diverted the overload beyond the basic five senses. Her familiar environment, so much a part of her, stretched and warped around her as she forced her feet and legs to react; her elbow painfully catching the frame of the bedroom doorway as her proprioception scrambled to meet the sudden new demand.

"Parents home calling".

The displayed words and accompanying lifted receiver icon shimmered with the same foreboding as the sound of the ringer; that at least mercifully silenced as Bethany answered the call.

The distress in Sheila Sawyer's voice replaced the last vestige of doubt with the deep, leaden-stomach coldness of reality.

"Bethany, it's... It's your dad. It was his heart; he's gone, darling. You need to come home. Not tonight; you'll need to pack some things and it will be too late. I don't want you travelling on your own late at night after hearing bad news anyway. But as soon as you can in the morning."

Details of the hallway, the least personal space in her home yet suddenly poignant in the urgent requirement to leave it, rushed at the sensitised portals of her shock-widened eyes. A fleck of ivory paintwork hung partly peeled away above the bathroom door. A tiny brown spider inched nonchalantly along the skirting board. A fine crack snaked from the light fitting to the patch where an old battery-powered smoke alarm had been before the mains one, blinking its redundantly calm green light, was installed.

In the ordinary space between rooms, a gap opened up severing worlds.

3

Leaving

Bethany had not expected to sleep; she had no recollection of having fallen asleep, but the jumble of images she remembered from her dreams told her that she must have. Her cabin size suitcase stood next to her wardrobe, the sight of it bringing back the packing the night before after her shaking hands had put down the phone. Clothing for a traditional funeral was clear in its parameters, but what was appropriate for the time in between? Dismissing some of her favourite go-to comfortable items as too casual, light or cheerful had, strangely, proved to be one of the moments when her emotions came closest to breaking through.

She went into the bathroom, hurrying through a basic wash. At least she didn't have to worry about packing toiletries; she kept a supply of those at her parents' house for whenever she stayed over.

No: not her parents' house. Her mother's house.

Her HRT patches though, and the diary she kept herself right by, noting for reference when she used each type of patch and when she had a period-like withdrawal bleed. She mustn't forget those. And she must be sure to take a photo of the August page on her calendar, since she wrote some of the things she needed to remember on that; years of familiarity and more presence than a transient reminder notification on her phone which she may or may not receive at a time when her phone was not on silent and when she could action it immediately.

Should she take a photo of the September page too, just in case she was still away?

Surely she would at least get to come home briefly before then. But this was new. She was leaving the sanctuary of her own surroundings without a defined return date.

Tears came crawling, aching behind her eyes.

How selfish. What was wrong with her? Her father had died, and what brought the tears on was having to leave her flat for an unspecified length of time?

Anyway, she couldn't be off work indefinitely, even adding sick or unpaid leave after bereavement days. Yes, she would be home well before the end of the…

Work! She hadn't let Magnus know. It was only 7am; he would not receive her text for a couple of hours yet, but that wasn't the point; she had almost forgotten to send one.

Her mother needed her to do better than this.

She should eat something before travelling. That was sensible, not self-indulgent. Wasn't it? A rumbling stomach would not be seemly in a house of grief. The thought sparked an unexpected laugh, quickly stifled as she awkwardly brushed her hair, unable to meet her own eyes in the mirror. She made her way through to the kitchen.

Ugh. The perishables in the fridge; she was going to have to throw so many of them out before she left, or else come back to see what had gone off. Might her mother be able to use some of it? She could wrap things in newspaper and use the cool bag she kept things in when she defrosted the fridge. Her mother wouldn't be feeling up to shopping anyway. Of course good people brought supplies to the bereaved. But turning up to the house with a picnic in a bag covered in a jolly dancing snowman pattern? Really?

What were the social rules here? Her instinct was to prioritise practicality over etiquette. She tightened the lid and tied the three quarters full plastic bottle of milk in a bag, wrapped up an unopened packet of ham and half block of cheese and scooped up the rest of a multipack of chocolate desserts which she knew her mother also liked. The rest of the chicken slices would have to go; the butter should last OK. Oh - the bread! That would have to go too; it would have been stale after a couple more days anyway. Should she put in the rest of the cake bars? Those were individually wrapped and would keep, but they could be useful to put out when people called to pay their respects. But she was spending too much time on this now, and she still hadn't eaten.

She forced down two slices of toast and binned the rest of the bread. Crumbs threatened to catch in her tight, dry throat even with the lubrication of butter; she forced herself to sip water as she ate, the crunching of the toast in the silence of the flat feeling disrespectful in its everyday mundanity.

Right. Dishes washed; toaster crumb tray emptied now that it has been given time to cool. Next thing: get dressed. Then check everything has been tidied away, switched off, unplugged as appropriate. Take the rubbish out. Oh; better take that photo of the calendar page beforehand. She had already thought about that several times but not done it. Text Magnus quickly first.

What was she *doing*?

Her *father* was *dead*!

Should she phone her mother, or just get away as soon as possible? She had already bought an anytime single train ticket on her phone. Her mother might be sleeping; surely she too would have been awake most of the night. Bethany did not want to wake her with a spurious phone call just as she had fallen into an exhausted sleep.

What were the rules here?

She took out the rubbish and recycling, bizarrely shocked by the complacent sameness of outside. Checked around her flat one final time. Picked up her phone to put in her handbag... *Charger!* Good God, that was a close one. Stashed the important item hurriedly in her case, shaken at such a glaring lapse. She had a bereft mother to support! She must do better!

Bethany said out loud "I am locking the door" as she did it, to seal it in her memory that she had. Tried the handle to further reassure herself that she had done it properly.

Time to go. Each step down the stairs to the main door pulled her heart on a matching downward trajectory in her chest. This was real. This grim milestone, so often imagined in nebulous shades of unknown; here, now, this was it playing out.

Everything was normal. Perth was calmly, stoically beginning another weekday. Shutters flew up on an opening vape shop, startling her; the energetic lilt of the ubiquitous 'How are you?' exchange between a couple of sociable morning people bounced its brisk soundwaves somewhere off to her right. Pigeons amiably dissected last night's takeaway litter on the High Street, cooing as a casual breeze fluffed their feathers and turned chip papers into listless white flags, surrendering the last vestiges of replete night time to a mundane new working day.

"...cannae be that bad?"

Was that question for her? Bethany looked around, jarred by the closeness of the words coming from somewhere she had not been looking; unexpected, the direction from which the voice had come eluded her. A man smoking a roll-up in the shadowed void of a doorway to a long since closed down shop. Ah, yes; the twist of mockery to his mouth amid a mess of dark red facial hair, the tilt of his head towards her, the challenge and judgement in his glinting eyes. Had she been subjected to *that* putdown yet again, when for once in her life she had an answer to knock the smug bastard for six?

If, that is, she could be sure enough of her senses to trust them to have read the situation correctly.

"What was that?"

"Sorry darling; no offence."

"No; I didn't quite catch what you said."

"I just said 'cheer up; it cannae be that bad'. You looked miserable."

"Right. Well, pardon me but you'll need to forgive my aesthetic shortcomings today; you see, my father has just died."

"Oh! Shit, I'm so sorry! Oh, f... I didn't mean..."

"So what did you mean? When you tell a complete stranger they look miserable, there are two possibilities. One: something has happened and they have every right. Two: it's their neutral expression and you have basically called them ugly. Either way, it's a dick move."

"Honestly, darling, I'm sorry, I just thought you were..."

Bethany held up her hand, palm outwards.

"Enough. I am not your 'darling', and I couldn't care less what you thought. If you are sorry, I hope you will learn from this and not say that to random strangers in the street ever again. Never mind me; learn the lesson in honour of my dad. He had class and he treated women with dignity and respect. You might want to try that some time."

She turned on her heel, leaving the psychological intruder's ineffectual sputtering behind her.

Concentrate! She was out in public; additionally vulnerable; exposed. She must focus, or else she would be well and truly punished by karma for her stolen triumph. She would either mess up through being distracted or find out an unnoticed, maddening mistake. *Think about something constructive.* She came to the end of Scott Street; crossed over South Street then the long pedestrian crossing spanning three sections of one way road outside 'Number 3'; the Autism Initiatives Tayside one stop shop. She cast a fond look at the blue-grey building which narrowed to the apex of a triangle at the end of King Street; glimpses of warm colours in the windows, snapshots of times when she found support and solidarity so close to her home. Pushing through the tight clench of sadness at having to rush away from it, her grim sense of battling alone brought her anger at the heckler back to the surface as she headed up Leonard Street towards the station. She felt her face burn with the rush of blood as her emotions roiled in the inner storm. *Get a grip on that or you'll get more hassle.* She forced herself to pay more attention to her surroundings. *Side road! Check for traffic; do not be that ditzy liability!* Losing any semblance of being in the right would be the least of all the risks if she failed to keep on top of that basic life skill. Giving herself a stern mental shake, she forced her mind onto her surroundings as she pulled her suitcase across the exit from the car park outside the imposing Radisson Blu hotel, its magnificent past as the Station Hotel irrevocably embedded in every block of elegant reddish-brown stone. Walking around the last curve of footpath, she stopped to get out her phone and prepare the ticket on screen for the ticket barriers at her usual place where she could avoid being in the way of other travellers to do so; next to the post box outside the fire exit of the station's coffee shop and newsagent.

The sight of the post box reminded her; did she have any birthday cards to send in the next couple of weeks? Unlocking her phone, she went to open her photos app to check the...

Calendar.

She had never managed to remember to take that photo of the wretched calendar, despite thinking about it so many times when she was so close to it but in the middle of doing something else. Forgotten, over and over again, in the minutes or seconds it took her to finish that something else. Now, too late, as well as the agonising realisation she had the stress of wondering what she might miss because of not having that information with her.

Oh for f...

Teeth painfully clenched in frustration, she raised her eyes to an impervious, glaring white sky. So much for getting the upper hand in those all too brief minutes with the intrusive stranger.

Still in public; appearance to be maintained! She opened the travel app, activated her ticket and gathered herself to get to the first of her two trains; the express from Aberdeen which would take her to Stirling for her connection to Cambusmenzie.

4

Journey

The caramel cheesecake brown and cream of Perth Station slipped away past the train windows. Bethany had a double seat to herself. Pulling down the refreshment tray, she set out her phone and Railcard; there was no sign yet of the guard so she minimised the screen with her ticket and checked for any messages. Nothing from Magnus yet; it was a tad early for him to have his work phone on. There was a message from her cousin Sharon, but best not get distracted by that until the interaction of showing her ticket had been coped with. Sharon was Bethany's most supportive ally among her relatives; she lived in Inverbrudock and it was she who had introduced Bethany to Diane after having become friends with her when Diane was making some enquiries about local history.

"Right then, all you lovely people; let's see your tickets and your best morning smiles, not necessarily in that order!", boomed a strident voice from the end of the carriage.

Oh, no. This was all she needed. Tristan was one of the regular guards on this route and well known for his witty repartee; he took no prisoners if people were not quick enough to keep up, but the overwhelming capable majority seemed to love it and regularly praised him on social media for brightening their day. Bethany could understand people appreciating a bit of comedy and welcoming the paradigm shift away from strict professionalism to a more friendly approach, but Tristan had a tendency to take it further than she could condone or was able to feel safe with - to other people as well, not only her. Confusing foreign passengers with his rapidly spoken, banter-laden announcements and making a dyslexia joke after having read out an incorrect departure time which saw a couple almost get left behind after getting out to stretch their legs on the platform were recent examples. The first time he saw Bethany's dark blue hair, a social defence she had constructed to try to channel the various ways her differentness was remarked upon into one predictable first bastion of othering, he had made a reference to the blue beings from a popular comic franchise; it was as though he believed he was the first one to do so. Telling him that no, she was the secret love child of the blue-quilled hero from a 1990s video game instead of giving the embarrassed giggle he had undoubtedly expected from her had shocked him so much, the logistics of her having been born in the 1970s had escaped him as a source of points to score and her next prepared line about time travel had not been needed. He had been inclined to scan her ticket as quickly as possible and leave her alone after that; he nonetheless managed to make her feel devoid of a personality and she never felt comfortable on a train he was working. Knowing that the tide of popular opinion was high in favour of his way of interacting heightened her sense of being prey without defence or shelter. She rotated her shoulders, trying to get rid of any visible tension.

The beeps of Tristan's scanner came closer amid the torrent of bonhomie. Bethany turned and held out her phone and Railcard, what she hoped was a passable smile fixed in place; she drew breath to force out an authentic enough cheery greeting.

"Hi Alison; is this you skiving off?"

Great; so he knew the person across the aisle. He was going to be stood next to Bethany's seat, holding who knew how prolonged a conversation. Would she end up having to ask him to let her out to get off at Stirling for her connection?

Use your brain, Bethany. He'd have to move before then to be ready to release the central locking for the doors.

Yes, but I need my ticket checked well before we come into Stirling so that I can get my phone and Railcard safely put away and not drop them when I'm also holding on to my bag and case.

Which is fair; sensible and reasonable. So if it comes to it, say that to him!

That's all very well, but it's essentially giving him the go-ahead to foghorn to the entire carriage about me Needing Assistance or Watching Myself Getting Off. Despite my demonstrating that I know what precautions are needed out and about and intend to take them. But that's not the part all the other passengers would overhear.

Internalised ableism alert!

Or not wanting to be advertised as vulnerable to a bunch of strangers going in the same direction as me?

Many disabled people don't get a choice in that!

True, but that doesn't make it OK and I am responsible for defending my own boundaries, safety and security.

Bethany's stomach churned. Seriously, why today?

"Good morning to you, young lady! Ah, so you're heading to sunny Cambusmenzie?"

Now, *that* was funny; it almost made up for the oozing condescension of 'Young Lady'. And at least he hadn't trotted out the 'Costa Del' line; that was getting irritating. Especially when he used it about places which were nowhere near the coast.

OK, she had to concede she was getting grumpy and pedantic now. *Find some thankfulness. Give the guy a chance.*

Think of something witty to say, something amusing without being barbed, about 'Sunny Cambusmenzie'. Heatwaves? Bikinis? Oh hell no; don't tempt him to sing hideous novelty songs. Sun cream? Hitting the electric beach before...

27

It was no good; this was taking too long. She had nothing.

"...better watch this one doesn't make you miss your stop, Alison; she never shuts up! Ah well, they say it's the quiet ones you have to watch."

What the *actual fuck*? He was not only lampooning her but inciting another passenger to join in?

"Come on, Tristan, take it easy"; Bethany recognised Alison now. She was one of the other regular guards, who did her job in an equally friendly but much more accessible and empathic way. "Not everybody wants to…"

But she did want to. She simply couldn't; not to Tristan's high octane rapid-fire standard. She wished that were allowed; that it didn't have to bring so much hurt on top of a crisis like this!

"My dad's just died! That's why I'm not full of happy chitchat about going to Sunny Cambusmenzie; I'm on my way to support my devastated mother!"

"Oh my God! I am so sorry. I didn't realise… When I said that about sunny Cambusmenzie I was just…"

"The 'sunny Cambusmenzie' part isn't the problem! Judging me for not being able to find the damned words when I need them; when I'm going to be humiliated if I can't match the speed of your gale force personality which should have a Met Office wind warning on it, that's the problem here. And trying to get your colleague to join in! Of course you didn't realise about my dad, and I don't suppose you mean any harm. That's kind of the point, though; you don't know what's going on in people's lives. Aside from the bereavement, there are reasons why I'm not good at matching your barrage of witticisms. I'm not going to declare them out loud in a public place; it isn't safe or appropriate, but do you know what? I'm forty-eight years old and I'm only now beginning to come to terms with the fact that not one of those factors makes me inherently bad or faulty. And the reason it's taken me so long is because of a lifetime of feedback like you've just given me, or more precisely given someone else *about* me as though I weren't there. Alison, I'm sorry you're being dragged into this. I was preoccupied and hadn't recognised you before, otherwise I would have said hello."

"Oh, please don't apologise, and I am so sorry for your loss. Tristan, you need to dial it back a bit. This is exactly why."

"But people like a bit of cheeriness; who wants everything to be sombre all the time?"

"You can be cheery and friendly without putting pressure on people, though! Alison isn't sombre! Let me put it this way; I would never go to a comedy show at the Edinburgh Festival Fringe and if I had to, I definitely wouldn't sit in the front row. I would know that there was a good chance the comedian would target me; it's understood that if you go to a gig like that and put yourself where the spotlight is likely to be, you're accepting that risk. But this isn't a comedy club. People are here because for whatever reason, not always a happy one, they need to get somewhere. And they're a captive audience; they can't get away. At least at the comedy club, they could get up and walk out, though they'd get booed for it. Every time I get on a train and hear you, I feel physically sick because I'm trapped with the prospect of impending humiliation. It may be harmless fun to you, but like Alison says, you need to dial it back. You need to think a bit more about the bigger picture, that's all. I don't mean never crack a joke. Just read the room a bit better."

"Well, I had no idea anyone could feel like that because of me having a bit of a laugh doing my job."

"But Tristan, people can, and there are a lot of them who wouldn't manage especially in the high pressure of the moment to put it across as clearly and constructively as…"

"Bethany."

"As Bethany has. And thank you; that was a lot of emotional labour for you to have to do, particularly at a time like this."

"I appreciate you saying that, Alison."

Dunblane Station appeared fleetingly through the windows of the train, jolting Tristan's attention back to what he was supposed to be doing; he waved a bemused apology and hurried off to check for any more tickets from Perth before the busy interchange of Stirling, now fewer than ten minutes away.

"And how are we this fine morning? Don't look so worried"; his jocular voice floated back through the connecting door from the next carriage. Bethany and Alison exchanged looks; the off-duty guard shook her head and raised her eyes to heaven.

"Yep; that's another one that needs to get in the bin. Some people's neutral expressions get picked on all the time; I get that too and it's exhausting", sighed Bethany. "Thank you for backing me up there."

"No problem at all. You know, we need voices like yours on passengers' user groups. I know this isn't the time, but if that's something you'd be interested in, give me a shout next time you see me. You go to Inverbrudock quite often, don't you?"

"Yes; my cousin and my best friend both live there. Oh, that reminds me; Sharon, that's my cousin, had sent me a message before my ticket and personality inspection so I should read it and get back to her, and I need to check if my boss has received my text too. I heard about my dad late last night. But thank you so much for suggesting that, and yes, I'd be interested some other time. At least to feed back to the groups if not join them."

"Of course. Well, look after yourself; I will be thinking of you. It's a tough time, but you're doing the best you can."

Why couldn't more people be like Alison? Well, thought Bethany as she checked her phone, at least she had wonderfully supportive messages from three people who were. She sent quick holding replies to Sharon, Magnus and Diane before gathering herself to leave the train.

The connecting service to Cambusmenzie was mercifully quiet in this direction at this time of day. Bethany was so relieved to be out of range of Tristan's showboating, the train was almost at Falkirk Grahamston before the renewed dread of facing and adequately navigating her mother's grief began to gnaw at her. As the train slowly lurched over the points which led it onto the Cambusmenzie branch line, reality slammed into her as forcefully as if she had been standing on the track in front of it. This was it. This new rearranged version of her lifelong background, strewn around a gaping sinkhole of loss in which she had to instantly assume a new role with vastly increased responsibility, was her present and her future; no time, no way to go back and prepare for this transition.

The train glided inexorably to a queasy halt alongside the single platform; the green light around the 'Door Open' button seared laser-like through the last seconds of detachment. Bethany almost forgot she needed to press the button.

Sort your head out! Extra processing time is a luxury you don't have any longer!

This new *now* weighed down her feet; beat the stressed tautness of her stomach like a drum; sucked the air out of her lungs; blurred her eyes and roared in her ears as she walked leadenly towards the taxi rank and gave the address, which suddenly sounded unfamiliar, to the driver.

5

Family Home

Sheila Sawyer looked startlingly whole; Bethany had almost expected her to have jagged edges and empty space where she had been solid. She was dressed for visitors; a fitted floral top over smart navy trousers, salt-and-pepper hair brushed back out of red-rimmed eyes, a light sheen of blusher on pale cheeks and a muted dusky pink lipstick softening the determined set of her mouth. Yet she appeared somehow deconstructed, as though an internal framework had been taken out and replaced with a different material not designed to be load-bearing.

The inner scaffolding wavered as she stood when her daughter walked in.

The neediness of Sheila's hug crashed over Bethany, making her fight the instinct to stiffen against it. She distracted herself from the intensity by looking over her mother's shaking shoulder at the room; the same as when she last saw it; except, not.

Gerald Sawyer was everywhere by being nowhere. It ran deeper than his personal effects; it was the subtle ways in which everything was set up for two people. The positioning of chairs; the placement of coasters; the flattening of the carpet fibres where two pairs of feet habitually rested. The empty space on the sideboard where her childhood birthday cards had traditionally stood awaited the sympathy cards which would soon start arriving as word spread.

"You sit down, Mum; I'll make us a cup of coffee."

"No! Thank you, darling, but I need to keep busy."

Bethany got that, but what if anyone came to the door and saw her letting her mother run around after her? What would they think? She was going to have to take that on the chin; letting Sheila cope in the way she needed to had to come before Bethany's rejection sensitivity and terror of being judged.

"I'll take my case upstairs out of the way; we don't want it tripping anybody up."

"Yes, of course; thank you."

The trek up to her bedroom felt like checking into a guest house; every step tentative through the landscape of Gerry's house now without him forever. The building stood to attention, its private space now formalised into the setting for mourning, the gravitas of receiving visitors, arrangements, paying of respects. Even Bethany's own bedroom had the newly hushed air of a mausoleum; a waiting area for returning to a destination with the same name of normality but permanently changed.

She hung up her changes of clothes so that they would not be creased when she needed them, dug out the cool bag and took its contents downstairs.

"I brought some things from my fridge; they would have gone to waste otherwise."

"Ah, good thinking, Bethany. Sensible girl. You must have left Perth very early; do you need to phone your manager?"

"I messaged him. He sends his sincere condolences."

"Of course; I keep forgetting you can do so much more with your smartphones these days."

"I'll be able to do a few things online for you; you know, letting the pensions people, the bank, insurance and so on know about Dad. There will be things we need to do in person, but it does help being able to do more from home. Sorry; I know it's all so soon, so raw."

"No, you're right, we need to think about these things."

"Did the hospital give you a leaflet about their bereavement team?"

"Yes, they did. It's on the coffee table. Someone will telephone me when... I've told them that we have our funeral plans with Stewart Ross Funeral Directors, you know, the one on the High Street? So they already know to contact them when they're ready to release your dad into their care. He's in the hospital mortuary right now; the doctors need to confirm that they're satisfied his heart attack was the sole cause of death."

Bethany nodded, thankful for her mother's pragmatism.

"I don't want to upset you talking about these details, darling; I'm sorry."

"No! Oh Mum, you mustn't feel you have to look after me. I'm glad you can talk about it; please don't be afraid to say the words. Say 'cause of death'; 'mortuary'; 'coffin'; 'funeral'; 'grave'. We're adults. All these things we're going to have to face, we face them together. We shouldn't have the extra burden of tiptoeing around trying to protect each other from the facts."

"I appreciate you saying that, Bethany. I know it must be extra hard because, you know. Oh, what am I saying; like you've just told me, I mustn't be afraid to call things what they are. Because of you being autistic. I know it must be challenging in ways I can't imagine."

"Well, yes, in some ways, but my being autistic will be helpful in others. Every autistic person will cope according to their own profile of strengths and weaknesses, just like any other people do, and find different things easier or harder. For me, being able to focus on details because it will take longer for me to process and feel the emotions will be useful at this time. I might remember things Dad said which help us to plan according to his wishes. I will be able to look at things that you might find too distressing, such as sorting out Dad's burial clothes."

"Oh, that would be a weight off my mind if I could know you were able to do that without it being too upsetting for you."

"Yes, I can definitely do that. Right now, everything feels strange. I know I should be feeling nothing but sadness, yet it's not like that at all. I've thought about it; that sounds disrespectful and ghoulish, I know, but I've tried to prepare myself and plan for how it would be when this time came. But these cataclysmic events are never exactly how we imagine them. It's simply not possible to predict in advance how they will feel; the texture of those emotions and reactions. Even now, my mind is racing in a hundred different directions. People, processes, what's going to be changed. When is an appropriate time to change the name in my contacts for the land line here from 'Parents Home' to 'Mum Home'. Part of me says get over that hurdle as soon as possible, but it feels so disrespectful."

A tear trickled down Sheila's cheek, leaving an ephemeral trail of hurt through the brave façade of her meticulously applied blusher.

"God, how clumsy of me. I'm so sorry, Mum; please forgive me. It's just that we were saying about being practical and facing things. Oh, I'm such a…"

"Now, Bethany, let's not do this, please. I have just lost my husband. I need to be able to get upset and show it without having to reassure you and soothe your insecurity."

"All right, I know, I know! I'm *sorry*! I don't know how to get this right; this is new to both of us! Didn't you say a minute ago that you realised my being autistic will make this challenging in ways you can't imagine? Well, this is one of them. I'm crap at 'people'. I'm slow at working out what people need from me, and I take some things too literally. I can be too 'all or nothing'. I don't know how to cope or react appropriately when you change suddenly and get angry like that. And yes, I know that You Are Entitled; that knowledge unfortunately doesn't mean any greater success at navigating that unpredictability. Can we please agree that we've both suffered a major loss and are finding our feet, and not make this a competition?"

"Of course. I shouldn't have snapped like that, and I shouldn't have implied that the loss of your father comes second in any way. But you're right; this is new to both of us, and we're both going to get it wrong sometimes. I know it's a huge ask, but I need to know that I can make mistakes without having to worry it will damage you, and that you can somehow accept that you will make mistakes without it bringing on that 'all or nothing' impulse you describe. You didn't even make a mistake there. It is part of the healing process for both of us that we need to be able to confront these sad milestones, like this now being your mother's house instead of your parents' house. Like you said, facing it together. Which means allowing each other to have our vulnerable moments. And as for changing the name in your contacts, it's for you to decide when it's best to do that. If it's helpful to you to get it over and done with, then please, go with it. Your phone is part of your own private space; the only rule is to do what works for you. And you are not 'crap' at 'people'. This is what I mean; what we both mean, about 'all or nothing'. You cannot get this perfect; there is no 'perfect' with these times in life. It's hard, and it's going to be messy. I don't need or want you to be some flawless saint. I need my daughter; the real, complex person I know and love with my whole heart and soul."

"Yes; fair enough, I do understand what you're saying and what you're asking. My 'insecurity' is part of that person you just described and say you need, though. I'm not going to justify it; I'm leaving that there. You need me not to be insecure, or at least not to show it; I cannot in all honesty promise to deliver that consistently for however long without a hitch. But I will try to see past my instinct that I have no right to ever get it even slightly wrong with anybody and that I'll lose not only them but any right to be loved by anyone if I do."

"Oh, Bethany. Is it really that drastic; do the stakes truly feel that high for you?"

"Yes! They always have! But I promise I will work hard at bypassing that to support you."

"And to support yourself. That matters, Bethany; it honestly does. I promise you in return that I will walk alongside you and do the best I can to be an ally to you."

"Thank you, Mum. And you still make the best coffee in Cambusmenzie."

Sheila smiled as the two clinked their mugs together.

"Your dad was proud of you, you should know that. I know things were never the same between you after the way he reacted when you found out about…"

"Mum, you don't need to think about that now. I mean, not on my account. Of course you're going to be thinking about it. But please don't force yourself to talk about it and go through any more sadness than what is unavoidable right now."

"No: I appreciate your thoughtfulness, but I need to say this, to honour your dad as well as to do right by you. When you found out about our loss, and by 'our' I mean all three of us; we both handled it badly, but especially your father. I need you to know; we both needed you to know, he deeply regretted the cruel things he said. He never knew how to begin to make it right; he always thought there would be more time."

"Of course he did; that's the nature of being alive. Our brains are not equipped to know our own future and so we're programmed to act on the basis that we always have more time. It would be a very empty life if any of us had no regrets out of all the many choices we have to make; the paths we have to choose or decline."

"Indeed, and so sensibly and profoundly put, as is typical of you. But that particular choice was wrong and should have been different, without a shadow of a doubt. And when it wasn't, it should have been corrected."

"Well, as far as I'm concerned it has now. I can get on with remembering and celebrating my father for the good times." Holidays past; dinners at the golf club; the time Ken and Janice next door had their loft conversion done and one of the builders put his foot through the ceiling just as Ken invited Gerry up to see the progress. Memories shuttled back and forth, bringing fragile yet hearty laughter into the changed home.

"And every time your dad and Ken were having a cup of tea, for years afterwards, your dad would pretend to pick flakes of plaster out of his mug. I had to say to him eventually, 'look, I think that joke has had its day'. I was beginning to catch the occasional annoyed look and the laughter was becoming rather thin! You'd giggle at it, and I had to start shushing you. Oh, I'm sorry, darling; you were so shocked and scared to find that something which had been allowed before suddenly wasn't OK, and I got impatient with you for not taking it in your stride. I appreciate better now why things like that were such a big deal to you. You were only about eight, I think. Yes, that will be right; their boys are older than you and they were in their early teens."

"Yes; I remember them kidding me on that the loft was going to be a secret den for them and I was so jealous. I begged you and Dad to have ours done, remember?"

"I certainly do. In the end we had to ask Janice to take you up there to see for yourself that it was mundane storage space!"

"I was so disappointed. I might have ended up in therapy if Aunt Carole's attic hadn't made up for it!"

"You've been up there?! Oh; was that when you went to help Sharon with clearing the house when Carole sold up?"

"Ah; actually, no. It was one Christmas, when I was ten. I'd used the second floor ensuite bathroom and the soap was finished so I went looking for a new one. I opened a door I thought was a cupboard and saw the stairs going up. I know it was wrong to snoop around without permission, but given my fascination for attics and hidden stairs, I couldn't resist."

"When you were ten… wait a minute, I think I remember that. You were gone for ages and yes, I recall you saying something to Carole about looking for the bathroom supplies. I hadn't realised you'd been exploring up there though! And yes, I completely understand the appeal. So, was my big sister's attic a letdown like next door's, then?"

"Not at all"; Bethany smiled enigmatically, the memory still fresh after almost forty years, and too precious to the raw, intense little girl she had been to share it with her mother. Not even today, in this time of reinforcing their bond. "It had a proper staircase; if not quite a hidden one, certainly a surprise one. And a skylight. That was exciting enough for it to get a pass."

The back door flew open, startling them both as an elderly couple with matching ruddy complexions and bushy white hair bustled in; the man gave it a cursory, belated knock.

"Sheila, we've just heard! Whatever can we say… Bethany, darling, I'm so pleased you're here."

"Janice, Ken; thank you for coming over. We were talking about you too; what a coincidence!"

Greetings and hugs were exchanged. The couple always smelled to varying degrees of their three spaniels; it was never a dirty smell, but an earthy one which could be overpowering. Today it was surprisingly comforting despite Bethany's heightened sensory sensitivity; it evoked continuing life, freedom and the endorphin boost of a good walk in nature. At this moment, suddenly hit with a wave of overwhelm, hugging Janice Rivers was like taking the air on a woodland trail; she could almost feel the welcome shock-absorbing give of the soft ground under the firm grip of walking shoes and hear the satisfying pops of twigs cracking.

"I'll put the kettle on."

"Oh, please don't trouble yourself at a time like this, dear."

"It's no trouble. I was going to make another coffee for Mum and me anyway, and it's definitely my turn."

Janice's calm green eyes met her own briefly and the older woman gave a subtle nod as Bethany escaped to the kitchen, letting the comparative quiet wrap around her as the running of the tap and gradually rising whoosh of the kettle boiling soothed her. She looked around, mentally preparing herself for the sight of her father's mug on its usual hook; would her mother have moved it? Surely not yet.

No; there it was, its newly enduring stillness a miniature gut punch. Her breath caught; she forced her attention towards getting down two different mugs for Janice and Ken, placing them beside hers and Sheila's on a tray and setting out milk, sugar and teaspoons.

Should she move her father's mug? Would the empty space or a substitute be more upsetting to her mother?

It's OK to ask your Mum questions about what she wants and how she would like to go about things; you don't have to know everything instinctively. Sharon's advice in her encouraging message which Bethany had read on the train came back to her. Yes; she would ask her, once Janice and Ken had left.

How did *she* feel about it, come to that; about when to start putting away his things? Her instinct was to protect her mother from the multiple tiny detachments, even though she knew those were a necessary part of coming to terms. Yet her father was scarcely cold. Yes; it was much too soon for her to start moving things, or to have that conversation.

But how did she *feel?*

The kettle came to the boil as Bethany dug deep, trying to summon emotions which she was wary of disturbing. A few things at a time, perhaps; in a few days, and starting with less personal ones.

Bethany was abruptly aware of how terrified she was by the thought of taking down her father's mug anyway; she had done so without giving it a thought for so many years, but if she were to drop it now? No. Definitely leave it.

She poured the drinks.

No; this was not the time for seeking to connect with her stubbornly elusive emotions. Or to find herself thinking fearful thoughts about dropping cups. She had a tray of four hot drinks to carry without incident; that was enough to think about. Heat flooded her bringing sweat to her palms, right when she least needed it, at the thought of how off the scale cringeworthy it would be if she had a manual dexterity fail now.

Perhaps she could say she had changed her mind and wasn't thirsty; take her own cup off the tray and lower the stakes a bit? No; it would hardly make a difference. She was going to have to be brave. One foot, meticulously watched, in front of the other. Focus on one step at a time. Do *not* think about all the times she had chickened out of trying an unfamiliar café in case she had to carry a tray in front of people, with only her own drink on it. Check her route in advance; no tripping hazards. Right. Come *on*; people are going to be wondering why it's taking so long.

Deep breath.

Bethany picked up the tray and walked steadily forwards. She paused at the doorway to the living room, making sure of her position relative to the edges.

"Ooh, careful now; let me take that."

In what way had she managed to look as though she were not taking as much care as she or any person possibly could???

Pick your battles. Time and place, Bethany.

Flushed with shame, she allowed an eighty-five-year-old man to whisk the tray out of range of her perceived incompetence. Telling herself that it was natural for people to flinch at the newly bereaved fetching and carrying for them and to view such people in general as being situationally frail, she wished it were a convincing enough explanation to ease her mind from feeling that she had not only accrued yet another vote of no confidence from the world but failed her mother and dishonoured her father's legacy by appearing clumsy.

Once more, she heaved the burden to the back of her mind and stretched a taut, aching smile across the mask of her face. Extending a brittle 'thank you' towards Ken, she took her coffee and her mother's and sank back into her usual seat, adrenalin flooding legs which felt as though they were made of half-cooked spaghetti.

6

Registrar

Sheila wiped away a tear as she gently replaced the land line handset on its cradle. She accepted the cup of tea Bethany held out, a valiant smile struggling over the distant horizon in a sea of grief.

"Thank you, darling. That was the hospital. They were calling to let me know... Your father, they are satisfied that there is no need for any coroner involvement. They are sending the details to the registrar's office and we can make an appointment..."

Her voice tailed off. She took a shaky sip of her tea, focusing on the neutral brown comfort of the bland liquid.

"To register the death... Dad's death. Oh, Mum. Look, I can call them. I can manage on the land line with the TV on mute."

Sheila picked up the well-worn remote control, her finger finding the relevant button with the ease of habit. The background chatter of two small time criminals arguing over a bungled heist, a need to get away in the first car they could find to hotwire and the consequences they were about to face from someone ominously nicknamed Spike was abruptly silenced; the two men's irate hand gestures animated the screen in the corner of the room, momentarily drawing Bethany's gaze.

"Are you sure? Oh, thank you"; Sheila's eyes followed the same path as her daughter's as the silly comedy they had been watching at Bethany's suggestion to take their minds off the hard slog of bereavement admin for a couple of hours continued to play out. "Do you want it switched off?"

"No; muting it is enough, keep it on. It will be sad enough as it is for you hearing me make the call"; Bethany was happy to take the visual distraction for the sake of keeping a window open to a lighter version of the world.

"All right then; I do appreciate this." On screen, the criminals scooped bundles of banknotes into rough hessian sacks; one of them laughed as he ripped up an unopened letter franked 'IRS'. Sheila unexpectedly spluttered into her tea. "What was that quote again about the two inevitable things are death and taxes? I always thought there was a third thing, but I could never remember what. No, I think that was it; death and taxes." Her eyes darkened with the shadow of sadness crashing down again after an all too brief respite. Bethany's heartache at being unable to fix this for her mother manifested as a physical pain in her chest; shame seared a sharp line through it as she flashed back over how long it was taking her to fully learn not to seek reassurance from the other person to ease that pain. She determinedly pushed those unhelpful thoughts away, replacing them with the pragmatic balm of the task at hand.

"Cambusmenzie Registrars; Ann-Marie speaking, how may I help you today?"

Taking a deep breath, Bethany greeted the receptionist by name and explained her reason for calling. She grimly forced herself to focus on the genuine warmth in the voice at the other end of the phone, giving the requested details and jotting down the appointment time suggested to her for that afternoon.

"That should be fine for us. My mum is right here; I'm calling on her behalf. Could you give me a moment please, to check with her?"

Bethany glanced over at her mother, which brought the TV screen back into her line of sight just as it became clear precisely what sort of car the criminals had found for their quick getaway. Of course; what else would it be? Her sensitive imagination readily supplied the muted out screech of tyres as the long black vehicle rounded a corner at a speed for which it was most definitely never intended; to compound the dawning horror of awareness that her mother was watching this, the boot flew open and a coffin slid out into a chaos of traffic.

"Hello? Ms Sawyer?" The receptionist's distant yet immediately close voice carried equal urgency and concern.

"Oh! Ann-Marie, I am so sorry. You see, I suggested we watch a comedy film and we've got it on mute while I make this phone call and, well, something rather inappropriately timed just happened in it involving a coffin falling out of a stolen hearse!"

"Goodness! What an unbelievable coincidence!"; Ann-Marie's heroic but obvious attempts to suppress her laughter set off the same chain of reactions in Bethany.

"Could I... One moment please, I need to check that my mum is OK", she spluttered, barely conscious of Ann-Marie's hurriedly professional agreement as she looked across at Sheila. Her mother's shoulders were shaking as the action on screen shifted from traffic cops scratching their heads around the abandoned coffin to pick up the progress of the getaway. Bethany's heart plummeted for a moment before she realised that Sheila's reaction was not distress but mirth! She turned to reassure her daughter; their shared look sent them both into the peals of helpless laughter which so often bubble from the volcanic intersection of pressure and unexpected release, yet never fail to shock. Belatedly, the awareness that a patient Ann-Marie was waiting at the other end of the phone filtered through.

"Sorry! Oh God, you must think... She's OK. My mum. She saw the funny side, which is so good; my dad would have too, you know. He's probably looking down on us right now having a good laugh and relieved for her sake."

"Hey, don't worry; I completely understand! We often see people finding comfort in a bit of humour. What unbelievable timing though, that happening in the film; I'm glad it hasn't upset either of you!"

"Thank you so much for being so understanding. So, the appointment time; did you say three o'clock?"

"Yes, that's right. Is that OK for both of you?"

"Mum, is 3pm good for you?"; Sheila nodded, smothering her laughter. "Yes, we'll take it. I appreciate your help, Ann-Marie, and your empathy."

As Bethany concluded the pleasantries of the phone call and wrote down the appointment time, Sheila unmuted the TV. Police sirens wailed as the getaway scene accelerated; Bethany rolled her eyes and snorted with laughter as the inevitable greengrocer's stall was sent flying, spilling its quota of conveniently spherical fruit and veg to roll far and wide.

"There you go; that's your third element to the quote. Death, taxes, and the road getting its five a day whenever there's a car chase!"

She and her mother collapsed into more giggles before wiping their eyes, slowly calming into the returned acceptance of this transitional limbo time through which lay glancing seams of unexpected lightness but no express route.

"You're right in what you said on the phone; your dad would have appreciated that. So, 3pm? That's good; it gives us plenty of time to have our lunch and make a start on getting utilities, insurance and suchlike changed over to only my name."

The visceral pain of that harsh reality for Sheila lacerated Bethany's soul once again; her stomach clenched against the concept of even the lightest lunch as she braced herself to help her mother through the tasks ahead. The film continued unheeded in the background; a forgotten bastion of a normality which had no option but to wait its turn.

The upgraded entry system at the town hall clashed so badly with its old stone surroundings, Bethany wondered how they ever obtained permission for the brash metal panel with its futuristic blue circle of light around the call button. Still, she was glad of the system's in-your-face overtness as a green arrow pointing towards the door handle and matching illuminated instruction to PULL lit up to accompany the inviting buzz. She and her mother walked along the narrow, hushed and tastefully neutral corridor towards the reception desk on the left. An officer in a wine-red trouser suit and cream blouse emerged from behind it to greet them; Bethany recognised her as the person to whom she had spoken from the burnished gold-hued name badge which proclaimed 'Ann-Marie Gilfillan: she / her' in large, clear lettering. Taking one social challenge, remembering who was who, off the list at a time like this rang like a bell through Bethany's soul; indeed at any time in this complex world, was there anyone who didn't on some level seek oases of clarity?

"Hello; Sheila and Bethany Sawyer? Thank you for coming today; I'm so sorry that it's in such sad circumstances"; the formality of the occasion could not quite erase the glint of recollection in Ann-Marie's eyes as the surreal phone call played out again in Bethany's mind. The three exchanged discreet but unmistakeable nods of solidarity.

"Denise is the registrar who will be helping you this afternoon; ah, here zie is."

The registrar wore a strikingly beautiful belted calf-length emerald green dress with a pattern of tiny purple and orange flowers; Bethany felt a rush of gladness for the colours which spoke to her of the ongoing cycle of life and nature to which she could take solace from imagining her father and all loved ones peacefully returning. 'Denise Connolly: zie / zir' adorned the attached name badge in the same format as Ann-Marie's.

"Please, come this way; we're going into the Pine Room, it's the first on the left"; Denise's kind smile reached zir eyes as zie gestured to the two women to follow zir. Bethany's keen attention to detail admired the artistry of Denise's eye make-up; zie had achieved an effect of discreet smokiness which for all it was appropriately understated, she suspected it must take zir considerable time and skill to apply. She welcomed the sense of gentle, quiet ceremony as the three of them entered the designated room; somewhat lacking in the implied evergreen hush of its name, it nonetheless held a certain dignity in its corporate impersonality. Darkly shaded uplighting lamps in the corners formed a merciful substitute for the switched-off fluorescent ceiling lights; a computer sat on an unassuming, generic grey metal desk in the centre of the room and the pot of registrar's ink sat in elegant isolation on a separate wooden table off to one side.

Gesturing to Sheila and Bethany to take a seat on the faded grey office chairs at one end of the high-ceilinged room, Denise efficiently clicked through screens on the computer as zie explained the process. Zir voice held compassion and dignity as zie told them that the hospital consultant had emailed the medical confirmation of cause of death directly to their office. Zie went through everything which Sheila as the person registering the death would be required to check before signing the form to confirm the registration. Finally, zie gave them a leaflet about using the 'Tell Us Once' online service to notify several key statutory offices of the death through one process for which they would get a receipt. Denise asked if they had any other questions; after her mother answered in the negative, Bethany took out a folder from her bag.

"Denise, I hope this is in order but we both felt that when we're formally signing off on the end of my father's life, it should include an element of who he was as a person; the real Gerald Sawyer. I've brought his portfolio from when he first applied to study architecture; it was his career and his passion. He helped a lot of younger people starting out as well as unofficially mentoring my cousin's housemate in London; an architect from Ukraine starting over in the UK after fleeing from the invasion."

"Of course; that is a lovely idea! May I see?"

Zie handled the folder with reverence, turning the pages with care and respect; zir interest in the detailed diagrams and notes clear and genuine. Bethany sat back, allowing quiet minutes of unspoken tribute to her father's life in this stark room where its having ended was placed on record. A fan whirred somewhere; doors opened and closed; traffic flowed; life continued around them impervious to the solemnity of these moments. Sheila blinked misty eyes and squeezed her daughter's hand.

"Thank you so much for sharing that, Bethany, Sheila"; Denise gently closed the folder and handed it back. Zie returned to the computer and a businesslike atmosphere settled over the room once more; a printer stuttered into action, its routine mechanical noises an apology and a blessing.

The papers signed and instructions for ordering certified copies talked through, Denise showed them back to the exit. As with all unfamiliar or seldom visited places, everything looked different to Bethany on the way out from what it had on the way in; her eyes darted around, taking in every detail, praying not to mar this solemn and smooth occasion by making a cognitive mistake and losing goodwill.

A door opened further back in the corridor, beyond the Pine Room; footsteps hurried towards them from behind. Glancing around, Bethany saw a blonde woman in a dark jacket with a name badge in the same format as Denise and Ann-Marie's; her tired brain approaching capacity for the day, that was as much detail as it could manage.

"Denise! Oh, sorry to interrupt when you're with clients; could I check that you're free for the rescheduled meeting tomorrow?"

"Yes, Jane, I'll be there. Thanks for confirming; I know you're finishing early today. I hope your evening goes well"; zie smiled at zir colleague in a way which suggested the evening mentioned was a much anticipated celebration. Bethany smiled at Jane too. Life continuing; happy times for other people, subtly acknowledged, not rubbed in but there on the periphery as a reminder that happier times were always somewhere down the line. A now familiar jolt of guilt accompanied the realisation that she was relieved to have a reason not to be expected to do any reading between the lines; to have no duty to seamlessly insert herself to the exactly right degree into a social conversation forming around her, to find that balance between integration and intrusion. She returned the kindly pressure of her mother's hand on her arm and clutched her bag like a lifeline as the automatic door swished open, heralding a mundane bombardment of outside air.

As they walked towards the taxi rank, Sheila paused outside a small corner café from which drifted the aroma of fresh coffee; its keen caffeine rush, incongruous to Bethany in late afternoon, mellowed for the time of day by the addition of a definite hint of warm chocolate fudge cake. Her mother appeared to check herself, resolutely turning towards the road.

"Do you fancy going in, Mum? It's OK to treat ourselves, you know; if you feel like it, we should go for it."

"You know what? You're right. I don't fancy sitting in the house for hours until bedtime. We can have a cup of tea and get home in time for you to do this 'Tell Them Once' malarkey before office hours end."

Bethany smiled at her mother's use of the word 'malarkey', trying not to sound teasing as she explained that online forms could be filled in at any time and it would be actioned the next working day which was entirely reasonable but also show that she had submitted them on today's date.

"I would be lost without your knowledge of this modern way of doing things, Bethany, and I appreciate that you fill in these gaps in my understanding of it without making me feel like a dinosaur. I should have taken more interest in it when your dad was picking up the skill. Even if only the basics." Her eyes glistened for a moment; she blinked rapidly and smiled bravely at her daughter. "That registrar explained everything well too. It was such a dignified, respectful process. Almost like a memorial ceremony in itself. It was such a lovely idea of yours to bring along your dad's portfolio."

A young waiter with long dark hair tied back revealing several piercings in one ear came over and took their order for a pot of tea and a slice each of a mouthwatering Biscoff cake.

"I must say, though, registering your loved one's death in somewhere called the Pine Room? It rather highlights the loss, don't you think?"

"I hadn't even thought of that! I suppose because I love evergreens, I hadn't thought of anything other than the tree. But yes, you're right; pining, that is a bit near the knuckle."

"Well, at least they had clearly run a Hoover over the place since I was last in there. They'd have had a nerve back then if they'd named one of their offices after a spruce!"

"MUM! Miaow! Oh, I'm so glad we can have a sense of humour."

"Indeed; we do need to hold on to that."

The waiter brought their order.

"I've heard a lot about Biscoff cake; it's very popular nowadays, I believe. This is the first time I've tried it"; Sheila's eyes widened in affirmative approval as she tried a forkful.

"Internet portal forms and Biscoff cake; your horizons are expanding by the day!"; a flicker of something raw in her mother's eyes made Bethany regret her words as perhaps a stage too far. The future must surely need to be manageably local and bite-sized for such a recent widow. She hid her internal self-chastisement behind a mouthful of the unquestionably delicious cake, wisely letting the misstep and the moment go unmagnified.

A passing bank of cumulus cloud blocked out the already watery sun for a few minutes before returning the weakened light to the sky. The café door clattered open as a group of students came in, heading for the big table at the back where they tossed folders and satchels on the corner sofa. A third taxi joined the two already at the rank.

"I'm glad we came in here, darling. I enjoyed my tea and especially that cake, immensely"; Sheila gestured to the waiter so that she could pay and tip him before he got caught up with the student influx. Bethany smiled; her sense of being on the right footing subdued, but mostly intact.

They were OK.

"Me too. Thanks, Mum."

7

Nadir

"I really appreciate you doing this for me, Bethany"; her mother gave a watery smile as she checked for the third time that the appointment card was in her handbag.

A car horn tooted outside.

"That will be Sylvia now. I feel bad leaving you to do this and then be on your own all day; are you sure you're going to be OK?"

"Of course! It's a good chance for you to spend some time with Uncle Ray and Aunt Sylvia after your check-up; it makes perfect sense when they live so close to the hospital. Please do give them my love."

"I will. Poor Ray is struggling; he adored his brother and it's shattered him that your dad has gone first when he's... when he was the younger one."

"He's bound to be. You focus on them and yourself today; honestly, I've got this. The rank is right outside the funeral director's so I won't need to try to phone in the noisy street for a taxi back to here. It will be fine."

Bethany hugged her mother and avoided looking at the zipped-up plastic shape on the couch until Sheila was safely out of the door. She tried not to think about the cold, clinical details of what was going to happen to her father's best suit and waistcoat; to the shirt, tie, shoes, socks and underpants in the bag over which she had discreetly laid the suit in its protective cover. Selecting appropriate underwear for Gerry to be laid to rest in had been something for which nothing could have prepared her; Bethany had seldom felt as out of her depth in terms of expectations to know the right thing to do than in this most personal of final duties. Had she been alone in making the decision, she would have felt inclined to go with the ones her cousin Liam had bought him as a joke for the Christmas after he retired; golfing themed with a play on the concept of a hole in one, they had made all of them, especially her father laugh heartily that Christmas morning and she knew from seeing them in the laundry basket on her visits that he wore them. It had been a step too far for her mother to contemplate; Bethany had deferred to her and looked out a plain pair, crisply dignified and almost new; hoping that she was right in supposing that her father would have approved of prioritising his widow's distress over sending him on his final journey with his most intimate clothing being something which bore familiarity and associations of laughter. Her chest tightened once again at the thought of her cousin's jolly gift being simply thrown away. 'No point getting maudlin over underpants of all things', she told herself firmly, tidying it away in her mind with a self-soothing resolve to write down her own preferences in such matters and take away the additional anguish of guesswork for whoever would be tasked with preparing her own farewell.

    She picked up the land line phone to call for a taxi into the town centre.

    The amiable middle-aged driver's eyes held sympathy and respect as he helped Bethany arrange the bag and suit beside her on the back seat. His greying, neatly trimmed beard made him look older than the popular rock band on his T-shirt implied; the top half of a mobile phone poking out of the pocket of his faded jeans revealed part of a motif on its case which looked suspiciously like a cannabis leaf. Still thinking about her mother's need for formality, Bethany didn't know whether to smile or wince at his heavily tattooed arms brushing against the suit cover as he passed her the seatbelt to secure around it next to where she had secured her own, thankful that she had remembered in time to avoid a galling unnecessary reminder.

"It's fine if you want to put music on"; she noted him reach towards a button on the dashboard as he got into the driving seat and then hesitate. "I could do with the distraction, and my dad would probably say that there'll be plenty of time for solemnity when he's in the actual hearse."

The cheering swell of a contemporary guitar riff with a strongly perceptible influence of Jimmy Page filled the car and Bethany relaxed into a light, undemanding chat about music in general throughout the ten minute journey. As they pulled up at the rear of the High Street taxi rank, she paid and told the driver to keep the change and got out, meticulously checking for traffic before going around to the other door to retrieve her precious cargo. The driver, already at that side and with the advantage of his rear view mirror, was at the door before she could finish processing that she had definitely not missed anything and was safe to step out around the back of the taxi.

"Hey, don't forget your bags!"

Really?

How had she managed to present herself as shallow and scatty enough to do that?

So much for making her dad proud.

"I'm hardly going to forget my own father's burial clothes!"

"Well, *Miss*, I am very sorry! No need to take umbrage."

"I was checking that it was safe before I walked around into the road; I didn't deserve that. I'm trying my best."

Why did it always have to be like this; thinking she had done well, passed muster, only for people to think the worst of her yet again? She was being sensible, making sure of the traffic before stepping out. Had she been quicker, no doubt she would have earned a "Careful" or a "Watch, now"; if she had a pound for every one of those, Gerald Sawyer could have had a more elaborate funeral than

55

Tutankhamun. How was she meant to adequately honour her father and represent her mother in this exhaustingly ableist society where these judgements kept on coming and somehow she could never win?

If only she had thought to unclip the seatbelt from around the bags before getting out, that would have proved she wasn't about to forget them. But then they could have slid to the floor and that would have been her being clumsy.

Her eyes smarted and she felt her cheeks flush as she took the bags in trembling hands from the no longer friendly driver. Forcing out a terse 'thank you', she hastily reminded herself to pay close attention to the kerb as she hurried away from the car. She took a moment to compose herself before walking into the funeral director's. Placing the bag at her feet and draping the suit over her arm, she fished around in her handbag for her phone, intending to put it on silent. As she lifted it to access the button on the side, the lock screen lit up with a notification that she had a missed call and a voicemail.

Who was it this time; who didn't get the memo about her mobile not being used for taking calls unless it was prearranged and she could ensure she was somewhere quiet? How had she missed a call? It must have been while she was in the taxi, enjoying the rock music, before she became a pariah yet again.

Awkward with the suit over her arm, not wanting to crease it or risk any part of it touching the pavement, she gripped the bag between her feet and prudently closed her handbag which was securely worn across her body before unlocking her phone and holding it up to her ear, cupping her other ear as best she could to listen to the voicemail with as much ambient sound as possible blocked out. From what she could glean, someone called Darlene? Marlene? Parveen?, had called from her work's HR department and it was something to do with a query about an overtime form she had submitted. HR had a note on her file about not calling her mobile; making reasonable adjustment for her auditory processing difficulties. Was there any organisation anywhere that paid attention to these notes and didn't inevitably miss them? Some private bank in Brigadoon, perhaps. Or the office of the platinum level of some mysterious members' club in Tir na'n Òg. Some valiant bastion of accessibility which was exclusive enough, far enough removed from the everyday slog that people had time to read and notice these details.

Fumbling with her burdens and the keen awareness of the exposed public surroundings, Bethany rushed a text message to Magnus explaining where she was and that she had received the voicemail but had trouble making it out. There was nothing else she could do at that point; hastily stashing her phone back in her handbag, she turned to go into the building. She momentarily pulled on the door clearly marked 'Push', internally chastising herself for another inexcusable and logic-defying lapse in concentration as she thanked the universe for her having realised before anyone saw. This time.

"Hi!"

Oh no; that was way too flippant and mortifyingly loud. This was a funeral director's! Her usual overcompensating and lack of volume control was way out of place here. The carpeted hush roared in her ears.

"Er... Sorry. Hello. I have the burial clothes for my father, Gerald Sawyer, to hand in for the attention of Lionel."

The receptionist wheeled herself out from behind the desk, a practiced ease and unselfconsciousness to her movements which made Bethany ashamed of her own fish out of water blundering despite having an age advantage of at least fifteen years. The younger woman's neatly bobbed white-blonde hair swished with each push of her toned arms.

"Of course, I'll take those for you. Thank you, and I am sorry for your loss."

It sounded genuine too, and somehow original coming from this pleasant, confident person. Bethany cringed at her own tentative ways, the product of lifelong manual dexterity fails and terror of getting it wrong as she placed the suit across the receptionist's outstretched muscular forearms. She must not be a traitor to the community by adding anything to the exhausting day-to-day challenges of another disabled person's life!

"Thank you, Karli. I've got his shoes and accessories in this bag here too."

"That's lovely; thank you for getting all of that together. Lionel is with another client at the moment but if you'd like to follow me, please, we'll put your father's clothes safely in the office."

Karli pushed the pad to open the door which led off behind the reception area; the action jogged Bethany's memory of there having been an identical pad at the door she had attempted to pull. Not that she would use the pad when she didn't need to, but shame flooded her at not having noticed it at all. She really must get better at keeping her wits about her and managing with the aplomb that Karli had clearly mastered. Bethany was not naïve enough to imagine that this poised, self-assured woman would not regularly encounter inaccessibility and ableism too, but she could hardly picture her making a hash of things and accumulating enemies the way Bethany so often did.

Setting down the bag next to the suit, she took the moment of stillness which Karli tactfully afforded her by backing up and turning her wheelchair quietly towards the door and waiting. She bade a silent goodbye to another part of her father's time in this world, then followed Karli back to reception and thanked her once again. This time, she remembered the correct way to open the door; before she could feel too smug about that, she realised that in the distracting panic of the unexpected voicemail she had forgotten to put her phone on silent as intended. Just as well no notifications of any kind had come through, then; it was no thanks to her that the sanctity and orderly respect of the funeral directors' work space had not been disturbed.

Free of the added demands of carrying bulky precious items, Bethany took a deep breath to steady herself as the everyday sights, sounds and smells of the busy town centre rushed in upon her once more. A green delivery van pulled up outside the closed Chinese restaurant over the road; its contrast with the red and gold frontage bizarrely reminded Bethany of Christmas, bringing a wave of awareness of how unexpectedly different that was going to be from now on. The town hall's clock chimed at the end of the road.

There were three taxis at the rank; her peripheral vision registered someone approaching the front passenger door of the first one, so she walked over to the car behind it. The rear door was locked, or was it merely stiff? Reluctant to force it and risk damaging it, she tried again; squinting against the reflections of the street in the car windows, she dimly made out the driver pointing forwards, animating the gesture to get her attention. Ah; they must be asking her to get in the front. Cautions about women's security travelling alone in taxis tapped their own internal alert against the chaotically reflective windows of her busy mind; should she be complying with that? She would have to open the indicated door in order to speak to the driver though, to ask them to unlock the rear door for her.

She couldn't get the front door open either.

The all too familiar metallic tang of adrenalin caught the back of her throat, crawling in pins and needles through her limbs and squeezing her heart and lungs with a clammy grip. What was she missing?

She bent to look through the window at the driver, who kept on pointing forwards, increasingly strident in his gestures. What was he telling her? Was she somehow trying the wrong handle, or part of the handle?

The car door was, by now, a meaningless block of two-dimensional colour. The components of everything around her were still there, but nothing was joined to anything else, in space or time. Nothing made sense. And this driver wasn't helping her; wasn't making any adjustment in response to the fact that whatever it was she needed to know, she wasn't able to get it from his gestures. He was just making the same ones over and over again, with decreasing patience.

She looked again at the door, and at the handle. There was nothing new jumping out at her. She tried one more time, then let go and raised her hands in the universal gesture of incomprehension.

The window slid down.

"It's the one in front, for fu… for flip's sake, woman!"

Bethany's world had shrunk in the fog of stress, shame and fear; its boundaries in the moment extended no further than this sole taxi and its front passenger door. 'The one in front' had only one possible meaning; an additional handle she wasn't seeing. Her hand felt for something which her eyes must be missing.

"No! The CAR in front! Jeez, what's wrong with you? Are you slow in the head or something?"

Yes. Clearly, the answer to that question was yes, and with no mitigation. Karli's competent, skilful manoeuvring of her wheelchair and her likable, sure demeanour floated across Bethany's tortured mind. She could walk; not to mention see; hear; use speech, albeit not always reliably. She did not have the type of diagnosis to which this man was broadly referring; although his attitude and language choice were wrong and discriminatory, she did not have the mitigation which would apply if his crude implications literally matched her disability. All of these privileges she had, and she was wasting and abusing them by managing to end up in this mess.

The memory of Alison the train guard's invitation to her to contribute to passenger user groups scoured her raw consciousness further. So much for her advocacy; some ambassador she was for disabled and neurodivergent people using public transport! Where had the wheels come off, so to speak; at what point had she taken such a wrong turn as to lose her wits and cognition this drastically? Sure, they always said they wanted people with lived experience of difficulties on these user groups, but not so ugly and dysfunctional as this; they wanted sanitised testimony which sounded no worse than anyone having a glitch on a bad day, the kind of thing to be described by whatever cutesy name was on trend for such things on social media. They wanted people who could tell them a ruefully admirable story and yet be relatable enough to join them in the pub afterwards without the risk of embarrassment. Not stories like *this*! Such undignified examples were for people to pass on in whispers under a cloak of shame for their heroic carers to stoically disclose while the individual stayed strictly out of sight! What was *happening* here?

Why, indeed, hadn't the taxi in front moved off with its passenger by now?

What was she missing?

"But somebody was already getting into that one; I saw them go up to the door!"

The man threw his head back and guffawed.

"That was the *driver*, you silly cow! He went to adjust his wing mirror! Are you on something?"

Ah. There was the crucial bit of information she had missed. Her peripheral vision under stress being one of the first elements of processing which her brain had to deprioritise, she had not picked up on the fact that the person approaching the passenger door of the first taxi had come around the front of the vehicle from the driver's side;

once that taxi was eliminated from her perception of what she immediately needed to engage with, she hadn't noticed what he did or where he went next.

It was still unforgivable, but becoming understandable. And as a bonus, that other taxi was available and was legitimately the one she ought to use; she did not need to explain herself further or have any more to do with this brute who was continuing to laugh at her, shaking his head.

She turned to walk towards the safety of the taxi in front.

Just as a couple laden with shopping bags brushed past her on their way from the Co-op; some sharp corner in one of the bags delivering a painful shock of a glancing blow to her hip. The world went into slow motion once again as they piled into the taxi in front; normal, carefree, capable.

The driver of what was now by right her unimaginably uncomfortable ride home was in such a state of mirth by this time, some part of Bethany that was still capable of rational thought wondered if he was safe to focus adequately on the road. This was too much.

"Ooh, unlucky! Too slow", he was chortling. "It's just not your day, is it? Well, are you getting in, or do we need to wait for your carer?"

"FUCK YOU!"

More howls of laughter chased her mercilessly as she fled, humiliated beyond endurance. It didn't matter where she went as long as she left the taxi rank behind; got away from not only this vile man but from the place where her father lay, betrayed and let down by her inability to do him proud but surrounded by people who coped so much better. Away from the streets and shops which were populated and visited by the people in her parents' lives; from their world, where she was failing them the most acutely at this crucial time. Cambusmenzie was small and parochial enough that people who knew her family would probably hear about her major cognitive lapse as a drinkers' folk tale in the local pubs. The blue in her hair, which she was allowing to fade out for the funeral but remained visible enough today and was normally a shield, would betray her identity.

Bethany ran; her breath painfully fighting to inflate rigid lungs, unshed tears straining behind her eyes and barring desperately needed air from her throat. Humidity turned her hair and clothes into abrasive alien material battling against her. She tugged viciously at her hair, glad of the pain; tearing at the frustration.

Past the end of the treacherous High Street; around the corner into the wider impersonality of the main road.

Too much. A stitch lanced agonisingly into her side; she clutched the solid mast of a bus stop, its metal cooling her face despite the muggy clutch of the air.

A bus stop.

A way out.

She had carried out her errand; she should do the responsible thing and go back to her mother's house. Not in that taxi; that was more than anyone could ask of her, but she owed it to her parents and the rest of the family to face returning to that rank. She would have to position herself somewhere discreet and watch for a different car to take its place at the head of the queue.

She dragged her reluctant, leaden body to face the way she had come.

That taxi may well drive past her! How was she meant to cope with that? She should; she would be expected to; she had messed up and she needed to face the consequences.

She had to find the strength. Dishevelled, her scalp sore from the anguished pulling at her hair, her entire body shook with the aftermath of her meltdown. The bruise on her hip from the impact of those people's shopping bag began to throb as she pushed herself to put one foot in front of the other.

The bus to Stirling came into view; a golden yellow mirage out of the greyness, its warm white lights calling through windows hazy with condensation. The fogged breath of people inside, being whisked in comfort to the lively city which combined an absorbing cosmopolitan buzz with a feeling of relaxed, small town familiarity. A place where she could catch her breath in her own time.

Rightly or wrongly, there it was; the bus looming large, too opportune to ignore. She reached out her hand; a benevolent blink of its indicator acknowledged her. Seen; answered; rescued.

The driver made a comment about the weather which filtered through as a jocular reference to Bethany's appearance; internal temperature control issues telling the world more than she wanted it to know about her physiological state when she least needed it. Compared to what she had been through in the past fifteen minutes, a passing remark as her ticket to Stirling was dispensed floated away into the realms of the inconsequential. On some level she was aware that it would have at least impacted a normal day, giving her a queasy journey; she gave wry internal thanks for the gift of perspective as she thanked the driver and took her seat.

Her phone pinged with a notification as the movement of the bus soothed her. It was a text from Magnus, replying to her message about the phone call from HR. He was concerned for her, most apologetic about the timing and quick to reassure her that there was no problem; merely a technical glitch with the overtime form, which he would take care of and ensure that the note about not calling Bethany's mobile was made more prominent. He thoughtfully confirmed that the caller's name would indeed have been Parveen, and that he knew from his dealings with her that she would be sympathetic and regret her oversight in making the call. He and everyone else at the shop were thinking of Bethany and her mother; she was missed and they looked forward to resuming work on the autistic hygge themed project with her and Diane whenever she was ready.

This was why she kept putting herself through all the bad times; the glitches, the humiliation, the not fitting in, being at odds with the everyday world. Diane. Autistic hygge. Belonging; togetherness; a base from which, with the right help, she could help others. Working towards a world where the next neurodivergent person to run into a problem such as she had today would have more chance of support and vindication at hand, to help them cope and to progress inexorably towards a world where the boorish taxi driver would be the one in the contemptible minority with his poor communication and customer care skills, his ableist slurs and his wilful ignorance.

Diane would get why things had gone so wrong for her today. She would understand every aspect of it; sensory, psychological, neurological, without the need for any laborious explaining. Diane would help her to move past the shame, the self-reproach, the comparing of her different but equally real disability and her life to Karli's, the disillusionment, the heartbreak of the setback. Diane would put her back together again.

Another flurry of messages, a few more taps of her phone screen, and Bethany's aching body and soul were booked on a train to Inverbrudock.

8

Sanctuary

"She was outside a fucking funeral director's, Des!"

Diane swiped an angry tear from eyes which brimmed with the intensity of rage at familiar injustice. Bethany watched from the couch; a deep orange cushion clutched against her churning stomach, her own movements dulled by the overload of the day's events as her best friend paced the floor, phone in hand.

"I mean, this guy had seen her come out of there. Did that not give him a clue that there might be a reason why she wasn't quite getting what he was telling her? Even if he had been clearer, did she not deserve the benefit of the doubt? I know I'm not making a whole lot of sense here; I'm not going to repeat the details of what happened, not with Beth sitting right here. As I said, it was one of those times when although the information is all there and the knowledge of what needs to be done, the processing of it simply doesn't happen. Or doesn't happen in what so-called normal society says is an acceptably quick time. Visual input is all present, but in meaningless blocks. Auditory input is there, and in recognisable words, but they don't form a coherent message. It all gets straight through; it's the coming together that takes extra time. And there's not a damned thing we can do about it. Throw in a vague, poorly constructed request and right on the back of it add laughing, the incredulous tone of voice and impatient body language and the result is a crisis. Especially when someone's already under pressure like Beth is."

Watching Diane dash away another furious tear, Bethany's hands began to unclench a little; her jaw to slowly refrain from the painful grinding of her teeth which she only noticed as it eased. As had happened so many times before, hearing Diane respectfully and eloquently describe the pragmatic science behind the incident which had made her feel such shame as she went through it alone and unsupported took away the worst of the pressure and paralysing horror. She was, however, still far from where she was supposed to be; she needed to get back to her family home. She had to face her mother after what had happened earlier. Lost in the vast mental interchange of replaying and anticipating so many fraught interactions, she scarcely noticed Diane ending her conversation and putting down her phone. Farolita stirring against her side as Diane petted her brought Bethany back to the present.

"Des is going to drive you back to Cambusmenzie; he's got the van right outside. It will get you back more quickly."

"But that's so out of his way! I'll give him something towards the fuel of course, but his time!"

"Honestly, Beth, you deserve it. I know you don't feel that way right now. Believe me, I get it. But you do. The way you were spoken and reacted to was wrong, and you're coping with a life-changing bereavement. Both Des and I will feel much better for knowing you're going back there in safer, more knowing surroundings. Des needs to pick up some supplies from a friend of his in Falkirk anyway; he can incorporate that into the trip. You need to let go of a wee bit of this huge burden you're carrying. Let your friends take a share; it will help you to cope and to move forward. You do not have to do this on your own. We get made to feel that we do, but it's a lie, based on ignorance and the invisible nature of our neurodivergence. People genuinely don't get it because they don't know how to see it."

Bethany set aside the cushion to let the purring Farolita climb into her lap as Diane sat down next to her. Stroking the warm, elegant curve of the Siamese cat, something finally uncurled deep in her solar plexus in response to the easy, unconditional therapeutic energy around her.

"It's so galling", Diane was continuing; "that what happened to you in one single and understandable instance of delayed processing is as much of a disconnect as the ongoing state of so many people's understanding of neurodivergent people. And that's despite so many of us being willing and having the privilege of being able to tell them our perspective in language they should be able to relate to, as well as the vast range of testimony from non-speaking people and all types of cognitive profiles. It pisses me off that despite all of that emotional labour from us, we're still at the stage of 'You can't be autistic; you're not like my cousin's landlady's five-year-old son'!"

Bethany, her humour coping strategy bubbling up through the slowly abating storm, had no trouble picking up Diane's cue.

"You can't be autistic; you're not like my cousin's landlady's hairdresser's five-year-old son!"

Diane's smile was a rising sun of solidarity.

"You can't be autistic; you're not like my cousin's landlady's hairdresser's driving instructor's five-year-old son!"

"You can't be autistic; you're not like my cousin's landlady's hairdresser's driving instructor's neighbour's five-year-old son!"

Both women shook with the washed-clean giggling of shared relief.

"You can't be autistic; you're not like my cousin's landlady's hairdresser's driving instructor's neighbour's postie's five-year-old son!"

"Aha! Logic break! The neighbour would have the same postie as the driving instructor."

"Damn! Yep; you got me there, you definitely won that one."

The entryphone rang through their laughter.

"That's Des now. I know you'll want to get straight on the road and chatting in a group will take a lot of what energy you've got left, so I'll leave you to go down and meet him at the main door"; Diane moved efficiently to the handset on the wall to convey this plan to Des as Bethany gently guided an empathically stirring Farolita to the warm space her human had vacated on the couch. Reluctant to leave such knowing sanctuary but increasingly dominated by the need to get to where she was required to be, Bethany kissed the cat's silky head then forced yet another shift of her overstretched mind as she checked her jacket, bag, phone and keys a second time. Performing a scripted, perfunctory farewell which didn't scratch the surface of all she was feeling but was the only feasible end to this visit, she touched every solid surface; door handles, walls, bannisters, to ground herself as she walked down the clinical bareness of the communal stairs to the main entrance.

9

A Burden Lifted

Des deftly whisked away a Chelsea FC scarf which covered the seatbelt socket on the passenger side of the well-used grey van. Forcing her gaze away from a worn patch at the side of the fawn-coloured leather seat, distracting herself from the automatic impulse to keep rubbing it, Bethany let her mind wander back to bus journeys in her childhood when she loved the novelty of being higher up than she would be in the car. A vague smell of recent coffee mixed with something less transient; earth after the rain, that was it. Brown smells; positive ones, not the unclean kind, blending smoothly with the visual interior. Fastening her seatbelt, she thanked Des once again as he started the engine and they pulled away from the sanctuary of Diane's building.

"Honest, Beth, it's no bother. I've been meaning to stop by my mate's place in Falkirk anyway and we'll all feel better for knowing you're safe and supported, not trying to travel on your own after what's happened. Don't worry; I don't expect you to talk about it if you don't want to. I know Diane will have helped you."

"She has. She always does. She helps me to reduce the impact of these horrible glitches and to reconnect with the good things in my life. Sometimes to see the funny side; there is no funny side to what happened today, but we did have a bit of a laugh. Well, we played a good spirited round of You Can't Be Autistic Minister's Cat, anyway."

"Sorry, you what?!"

"It's a twist on that Victorian word game, The Minister's Cat, where people take turns to describe the cat with words beginning with each letter of the alphabet and have to get the ever-increasing sequence right. In our version, it's about how so many people think that autism is restricted to young boys, and outright disbelieve autistic people because they're not like some more conventionally diagnosed young autistic boy they know of. So it starts with something fairly simple, such as 'You can't be autistic; you're not like my brother's boss's five-year-old son'. Then you take turns to add on another degree of separation, like 'my brother's boss's window cleaner's five-year-old son', until one of you either forgets the sequence or comes up with a logic flaw like, say, 'grandmother's daughter's five-year-old son' because you wouldn't generally say 'grandmother's daughter'; that would be a mother or aunt. We're not so pedantic as to take on all the potential complexities of blended step-families and lose the point of the game! It's one of our ways of getting our own back, harmlessly and therapeutically, on a world that so often makes us the punchline of some universal in joke."

"Ah, I get it! That's brilliant; it does show up that kind of ignorance for what it is, and as you say, without harming anybody."

"Yeah, though mind you, I was chatting with someone recently at an event at the Tayside one stop shop in Perth and as I often do I was kicking off about how hard it is for non-white and non-cis-male autistic people to be diagnosed because there is that perception of the silent young white boy sitting on the floor lining up his toys and the person I was speaking to said that I had precisely described their nephew. It was yet another social faux pas on my part and I hate myself for it, but at the same time I could accept it for the valuable reminder it was that those young white boys are no less in need and deserving of support. It's about growing beyond that demographic, but not away from it;

not to the detriment of anyone, especially a child, who needs that clarity and inclusion. The problem with me is that I have this maddeningly hapless tendency to make the right point to the wrong person. I validated everybody who's ever called me reckless and careless despite how desperately hard I try to get things right and do good, because I got carried away and didn't see the risk of saying that directly to someone whose own circumstances I didn't know. I thanked that person for the valuable reminder, which in the past I wouldn't have managed to do. I'd have gone directly to situational mutism; do not pass Go, do not collect any credibility! Since I had a crisis and hit rock bottom last year, I've become more able to turn these experiences into something constructive and I genuinely was thankful to have that reminder and to give that acknowledgement to the other person. But I was so afraid I'd harmed the image of the one stop shop by doing a social fail while I was there as one of its members. Fortunately, Matt, the Projects Manager for Autism Initiatives who oversees that and their other ones in the Highlands and Edinburgh, was there and he saw me bolt outside right afterwards in a panic. He came out to check on me and I confessed; he said that I shouldn't feel the need to take on that burden as the point of the one stop shops is not to cure people of being autistic and certainly not to get anyone to the point where they never make a mistake or where they instantly, in real time, anticipate every possible pitfall when talking to someone, because nobody autistic or not can do that. He reassured me that I hadn't let anybody down and that none of the staff would feel negatively towards me."

"Sounds like a sensible bloke. Diane's mentioned him too; he supports Chelsea, so he's obviously got his head screwed on! Seriously though, Beth, he's right; nobody would talk to anybody or gain any understanding of other people if we were all so cautious we never took a risk."

"True, but that's more applicable to deliberate risk; a calculated gamble which is a conscious choice, not unintentionally being a thoughtless social klutz."

"You're being way too hard on yourself. That's not a criticism; I know it's years of bitter experience and double standards and having to fight ableism that makes you that way. I see it in Diane too, and to a certain extent in my brother. Jason being hard of hearing has had to contend with people infantilising him all his life too. Going to the gym helps him to feel more in control and take pride in himself; that works for him, it may be that something different works for you and Diane. I wish we could take away the anguish it causes both of you, but I know, and Jason knows, that we can't. That to presume to do so would be minimising what you're going through. But you do need to cut yourself extra slack at the moment, Beth. Losing a parent is a huge event to process and keep going through."

"It hasn't only happened to me though. My mother has lost her husband. People have lost a brother, uncle, friend. But particularly my mum; I owe it to her to handle this perfectly."

"None of which invalidates your grief and your need for support. There's no pole position to compete for in order to deserve help when it comes to bereavement. You will be better placed to support your mum if you can take a bit of the heat off yourself. You did the right thing in the moment today; you went to Diane, and that has helped you gain the strength and belief you need to carry on. You need to take from that, that it's appropriate for you to need help and to reach out."

"I know, you're right. Mind you, this is going to sound so bad but there's a part of me that feels a certain easing of pressure because of the bereavement. *Not* that I'm in any way glad about it! But the fact is, I now have a socially acceptable reason to be a bit slow or say the wrong thing or not get something done in time or mess up because I got tired or distracted, or have a facial expression that someone takes exception to. I think that incident at the event has come back to my mind with added shame because it happened before my dad died and I didn't have that mitigating factor. Oh God, does that come across as having wished for a death in the family for my own selfish ends? Because it never occurred to me to think that way."

"No; it comes across as having been living with intolerable stress for far too long. Nobody can predict how they will feel when the time comes to face a bereavement which was always going to happen one day. Whether it's a shock as yours was, or the end of a long illness, you're bound to have all manner of feelings that will take you by surprise or seem at odds with what you think you should be feeling."

"Indeed, and the thing is, I knew that. I knew, in an abstract way, to be prepared for unexpected feelings and for nothing being predictable. Yet I still feel caught out."

"Again, that's your perfectionism kicking in, and your defence mechanism; needing to get one step ahead of a world which has always felt one step ahead of you. All of which is absolutely natural."

Bethany nodded, lapsing into a spent silence as the monotony of the main road lulled her into inertia. The shifting greys of the increasingly overcast sky pulled at her vision, draining her to the baseline flat feeling of so many days where ordinary life was sensory overload. Ah; something familiar at last in this surreal timescape!

"Look; a pie and mash shop van!"; Des raised a hand in greeting as the white Transit with 'Phil's Pie and Mash' and a London phone number on the side passed them in a swish of rain-slick tyres.

"Do Londoners really eat jellied eels?"; Bethany's random curiosity sparked an associative leap.

"Yeah; we do. Have you ever wanted to try them?"

"Eewww, no; they sound absolutely revolting!"; the words were out before Bethany could register the potential offence. "I mean, texture-wise; you know, with sensory sensitivity. I guess some autistic Londoners will eat them, as a cultural thing. We're not all the same after all, and there I go making everything about autism again"; why didn't she have a vocal brake pedal?

"Hey, don't worry; most people outside London, and some people in it come to that, feel the same. They're actually highly nutritious, jellied eels."

"If they improve social instincts I'll eat them raw!"; Bethany regretted her words for a different reason as her stomach lurched.

"Mate, if it would improve your ability to give yourself a break I'd eat them wrapped in tripe."

"Gross! But rather touching. Thank you."

"Honest, you're more likely to upset a South Londoner like me by calling them a Cockney than by not liking the idea of jellied eels. That's East London, but we all get called it when we're away from the city. I don't mean using it innocently in general conversation; more when it's deliberately used pejoratively."

Giving her the knowledge which would ensure she never made that mistake, plus the added layer of reassurance that she wouldn't have offended in the first place. No wonder Diane felt so safe in her best-friendship with this guy and his brother; her shepherd moons.

"I should message Diane and let her know we're well on the way"; Bethany pulled out her phone and composed a brief text. "She's been amazing. Not only now, but all the time I've known her. I can't quantify the help I've had from her."

"You've helped her a lot too, mind. You were the one to put the pieces together for her about being asexual and aromantic. Your personal experience was invaluable to her and you shared it with her when you first met; before you'd become close. She'll never forget that, Beth."

Perhaps it was the extreme stress of the day; maybe it was Des' position as a trusted friend but one step removed from the intensity of her closest relationships. Perhaps it was the added weight of bereavement making it unsustainable to keep on carrying years of a different, unspoken grief. Or maybe it was simply the soothing environment of comforting smells aligning with neutral colours in a homely van cruising along a bland road under the steady visual beat of the lamp posts passing the window that made it the right time and place.

"Actually, Des, I… I haven't been totally honest with Diane about that. Or anyone else; not even Sharon. I *have* been truthful about my being asexual and aromantic now and for as long as I've known Diane and you. I would say, with my knowledge now, that I've always been on the asexual and aromantic spectra. But I haven't always been without any experience of, well, in layperson's terms… I have been a liar to say that I've never had those feelings. I've vaguely admitted to capacity for romantic feelings; probably because romantic is viewed as more fuzzy and PG-rated than sexual and therefore less likely to get me into trouble so it's easier to admit including to myself. I don't mean to diminish the intensity and equality of romantic orientation compared to sexual; I don't hold with that hierarchy, but society does and that's what I've felt the need to protect myself from. Anyway, what I'm getting at is, I have held some things back. Des, I swear I have never been in a relationship; it's been unrequited on both occasions…"

"Bethany, I'm honoured that you feel able to share this with me, but please know that you don't have to justify anything. I may not be asexual and aromantic but I've learned a lot from Di and one thing I do know is that it is a spectrum, and that sexuality can fluctuate. You do not owe anybody an explanation or justification of your thoughts, and even if you had been in a relationship and kept that private, that is your prerogative. You gave Diane the benefit of your experience, and you centred her in that conversation. She would be the last person to think you owed her every fine detail of your personal history, and I highly doubt Shaz would think that either. It's entirely up to you how much or little you want to tell me or anybody else, but if it helps to talk about it, please do."

"Thank you, Des. That means so much. So, yeah, there have been two occasions. When I was a teenager, there was a youth club leader; a woman. I told one person; my so-called best friend, who couldn't resist a bit of drama and told her. She did not take it well. This was the late 1980s, you see. I was treated like some sort of predator. I was fifteen! And I hadn't done anything. I'd talked to my friend, as teenagers do. Looking back, if the woman had shown any signs of reciprocating, I would have run a mile. It was an escape more than anything else; there was the bullying at school, not fitting in with my own peers at the youth club despite having been pushed to join it in order to make that happen; the sensory overload and fatigue I didn't understand back then; all of that. Then when I was in my first paid job, there was an older colleague. A man this time; high up in the company but not directly involved in line managing me. After the way things were handled because of the youth club leader being so repulsed by not only a girl but a particularly awkward and dysfunctional one having Those Thoughts, at first I thought it was comparatively OK to have these feelings for a male colleague. This was the 1990s and we hadn't come as far as a society as we have now so yes, I guess I have to admit to internalised homophobia too. Everyone had such an added problem with the attachment in my teenage years in that the person was female. My parents told me how selfish I was for risking having that label on me and bringing trouble to their door. So this felt as though it would be less stigmatised, and because I was an adult and not in his department, I thought it wasn't wrong. I still knew I needed to keep it secret. I'd learned how repulsive I was from the way the woman reacted. That went way beyond the fact I was underage and her duty of care. I got the distinct impression she wouldn't have minded so much if it were one of the normal, popular crowd, of whatever gender. I don't mean that she'd have done anything inappropriate with any young person, but she wouldn't have been offended in the same way. So this guy at work, it was the same but different. I had all this guilt that I was somehow betraying the LGBTQIAP+ community by having feelings for a man. I always knew on an instinctive level that I didn't fit into whatever the hell 'normal' was in terms of experiencing attraction, before I ever learned about allonormativity and amatonormativity or about asexuality and aromanticism being a spectrum, so it was yet another group in which I needed to belong and fell short. I also felt that it would undermine my credibility to have to admit feelings for someone else after the intense attachment I had to the youth club leader, when I had been so distressed by the pressure I got to move on. I felt it would be giving people carte blanche to force me into anything they felt inclined to, because I'd proven them right and myself wrong by eventually having feelings for someone else. Unlike the previous occasion when I was a minor, I felt as though I would have entered into a fling, or something like it, with him if I could have been anywhere near his league. I knew I didn't want to live with anyone or be anyone's partner, but I did want something, and it was neither all physical nor all emotional. Looking back now, maybe I wouldn't; I understand my past better thanks to many an in-depth conversation with Diane about her own attachments which, she has settled in her own mind now, genuinely were all alterous. I have come to recognise that I was going through a similar psychological process in that the attractions were a false resolution to a different quest. I needed both a mental escape and a way to feel more connected; to know I wasn't the cold and aloof person I kept being told I came across as. I may have been the one to encourage Diane to recognise her asexuality, but she was the one who learned in more depth about the separate nature of romantic orientation and sexual orientation, and about alterous attraction which is something other than sexual and / or romantic but not strictly platonic. Hero-worship could logically be part of, or the root of, an alterous attraction. But those two experiences I had were not alterous. They were, I'd say, theoretically sexual, and certainly romantic. I stand by my conclusion that I was nevertheless on the asexual and aromantic spectra, because while I had feelings for each of those people, I had precisely zero attraction to any other person. When it was the youth club leader, I would no more have wanted any other woman than I'd have wanted a man, and vice versa with the colleague. The thought of being forced to replace them with anyone else 'more appropriate' caused real distress. Thinking back, I can see that perhaps the part of me that was looking for that high, since we're all bombarded with propaganda about it only coming from being conventionally in love, focused on unattainable people because I didn't want a sexual or romantic attachment at all and I simply didn't realise it at the time. My addictive craving for an emotional rush, enhanced by my autistic tendency to big feelings, shaped that high into the form I was conditioned to expect it to take, in the same way as the brain perceives meaningful images or sounds in random patterns. There's a name for that; ah yes, pareidolia. You know, when people see Elvis on their toast or hear messages when they listen to a recording played backwards. I'm not saying the *attraction* was an illusion; I'm saying the *nature* of it was. My feelings back then told a different story, and they were pervasive; they dominated every part of my life, like a watermark nobody but me could see. Years of keeping that secret at work; knowing that I would be punished in what I now recognise as the most traumatising way for an autistic person, being forced to deconstruct and painstakingly amend my every thought. To rebuild my whole consciousness at a molecular level with nothing familiar any more and no break from the exhaustion of that mental discipline, day and night, as I was when people found out how I felt about the youth club leader. Yes, I knew that I couldn't take it as a rejection that she didn't want a relationship with me; she'd have gone to prison. But the colleague was a different matter. He never found out about the extent of my feelings, thank Goodness, but we started out as cordial acquaintances and he seemed at first to respect my lack of conforming to the crowd but the more he got to know the real me and saw the glitches and mask slippage, the more he started to distance himself. It didn't help that as my feelings for him developed, I lost my grip on the English language and generally became awkward and useless around him. No wonder he was as disgusted by me as the woman in my teenage years had been. He made a show of gravitating towards a circle of favourites; the successful ones who weren't contemptibly beneath his level, and he'd turn his back or glower at me and move closer to one of them or smirk and roll his eyes when I walked into the room. Eventually, I began to avoid him and his circle; I carry sadness now about quite a few other colleagues with whom I could have had better working relationships, maybe friendships, if it hadn't all become so bound up with him. He moved on to another job eventually and that was that. Some would say it was a fantasy; I'm resistant to that because it feels clichéd and derogatory as well as uncomfortably heteronormative. I do however accept that from the initial rare attraction, I fell in love with *how it felt to experience that novelty and euphoria* rather than with *him*. Then, once the negative, unrequited, self-loathing vibe took over, I was in love with the *memory* of how that experience felt at the beginning. I still think about him; not romantically, those thoughts have long since run their course, but the inherent need to prove myself and impress him remained after that aspect faded away. Possibly because that was the underlying motivation in the first place; seeking absolution, as well as being lifted out of the constant dragging tiredness. And he has never been replaced, because yeah, I am asexual and aromantic. But he's so bound up in my internalised ableism, in that sense I cannot claim to be over him. Every time I have a glitch, especially a really cringe one like today, I have the added torture of imagining him watching it like a film or getting to hear about it. Scenarios play out in my mind, uninvited and unwanted but I'm too mentally drained to stop them, where he berates me or laughs about me with other people; more cruel than he ever actually was. So yeah, I have lied to everyone, including Diane and Sharon, despite all the support they gave me. I get what you say about not owing people my private thoughts, and that they wouldn't hold that over me as some sort of debit on the account of my interaction with them. But at the same time, I've actively lied to them about something fundamental and in Diane's case, relevant to aspects of her life she has bravely shared with me. It's not that I thought they wouldn't understand or that they'd judge me; it's more that it had become so central to my safety and to not having any more demands on my energy and encroachments on my space to keep it secret, I became terrified to tell anybody at all because I felt if I let it out after keeping it secret for so long, eventually I would choose the wrong person to confide in and it would all blow up in my face. Even though I'm no longer in that workplace and have no connection to that guy who moved to England when he changed jobs, the fear of it getting back to him and what he would do to me in retaliation for such an insult is as strong as ever. When you're fifteen and struggling with intense feelings, not knowing why they're too big for you because nobody's told you yet about autistic amplified emotions, and your own parents tell you you've forfeited the right to privacy because of your bad thoughts, that sticks with you and colours your adult attachments even though the moral and legal implications are different."

The quietness in the van as words so long unspoken adjusted to being out settled around Bethany like a weighted blanket as they turned off the main road towards Cambusmenzie. Des exhaled as he lifted one hand briefly from the wheel and ran it over his close-cropped dark hair.

"Beth, that's... Jeez. How could they, I mean I know I shouldn't disrespect your parents when you've just lost your dad but how could they do that to a kid? Mate, I am so sorry you've had to carry this on your own all these years. Your secret is safe with me. How do you feel now you've told me?"

"I honestly don't know yet! But I don't feel in a panic, which is a good start. I guess I feel I've made a step forward towards the day I can be honest with other people; at least Diane and Shaz. And Jason. I... Would you mind telling him for me? Now I'm going to come over as ableist in a whole new way because I think I was able to tell you because we're sitting side by side, not facing each other and you're driving - not that I'd tell you anything too shocking when you need to concentrate on the road! - so that gets me out of any expectation of eye contact or looking at your facial expressions as I tell you, but with Jason I'd have to be facing him so he could read my lips!"

"No, that's not ableist; I completely understand. It's allowed for people with different disabilities to have opposite needs in a situation. You're accommodating Jason by considering how to include him in a way which adjusts to his deafness. And that's if and when you want him to know. This is your confidential business. You are in charge of who gets told, when and how."

"This seriously is a weight lifted off me"; Bethany yawned unexpectedly. "Excuse me; that was like the Channel Tunnel! I don't know where that came from."

"It's no wonder, the rollercoaster you've been on today. You've taken an enormous step in telling me what you have. If you need to take a nap or just sit quietly for a bit, that's no problem at all. I'd be amazed if you didn't."

Bethany leaned back against the worn headrest, her eyes unfocused and drifting closed as the van neared more and more familiar roads. Des's trusty navigation software spared her the mental gymnastics of giving directions as they eventually covered the final local turnings and pulled up outside the house.

A woman in her late sixties wearing a linen top and trousers too smart for gardening looked up from tending her flower beds across the road as Des opened the passenger door for Bethany.

"Hello, dear; how's poor Sheila doing?"

"Hi, Ginty. She's bearing up, thank you. This is Des Asante, a friend of mine; he gave me a lift back from… I was sorting a few bits of paperwork out. Des: Virginia Flett, my mum's neighbour."

Des and Ginty exchanged nods; the neighbour's eyebrows raised, barely perceptible but recognised by those who had no choice but to become sensitised to such things.

"Yes, Sheila said you had to go to the funeral director's. Wasn't that this morning though?"

"It was. I, ah, got held up. A bit of a glitch with my taxi back."

"Right. You know I would have taken you if I were free, but I had another commitment today."

"I know! I wasn't making a dig; you were querying why I'm only back now and I was answering that."

Ginty unfolded her arms to brush a stray wisp of silver hair back behind her pearl-studded ear then leaned on her closed garden gate.

"People are there for you as much as possible, Bethany, but Sheila needs you to be strong and put her first. Don't imagine I didn't notice how put out you looked when I told you I wasn't free to drive you; if your mother hadn't been there I would have told you about yourself there and then. You need to take responsibility and face the fact that your own concerns and social life are going to have to be put on hold for a while."

"My concerns; by that, I take it you mean my autism and variable mental health? Because I don't have the luxury of putting those on the back burner. You're also making the classic ignorant mistake of trial by facial expression; getting instinctive anxiety too new to have been fully processed confused with a deliberate, preconceived attitude of entitlement. Look, Ginty, I appreciate that you've helped out with driving and your support for my mum, but I'm not going to stand here and justify myself any further in the middle of the street. I didn't take off on some social jolly; I had a problem, my friend Des helped me, and now I'm back. That is all you need to know."

"This is not the time for self-indulgence, dear. You need to be thinking of your mother now, not yourself. Or your *friends*"; she gave Des a sideways look.

"Ms Flett"; Des's voice cut with calm but steely authority through the dressing-down and the fog rising in Bethany's brain as his hands rested gently on her shoulders. "I don't know you and as you can tell from my accent, I ain't from these parts. But where I come from, when we rally round a bereaved family we don't pick and choose who to support and kick people when they're down. Bethany needs and deserves support too. She's had a particularly tough day, which is allowed. There is no pecking order as to who may and may not visibly struggle. She don't owe you any details and you've no right to judge her like this. Now, I'm going to see Bethany safely to the door. Please find some empathy before you approach her again."

He steered Bethany, by now on the verge of shutdown, around the back of the van and across the road. Trying the door handle with shaking hands, she was relieved to find it locked; she had gotten back before her mother. She had at least some time to regroup from this latest onslaught before facing her.

"Are you going to be OK? I can call my mate and let him know I'll be later…"

"No, Des, you've done more than enough. Thank you so much. I'll make myself a cup of tea and do a bit of polishing; that will ground me."

Watching the van disappear, she turned away from Ginty Flett's piercing stare and fumbled for her keys. The quiet in the house accused her, oppressive with none of the mercy of companionable silences alongside her friends. Loneliness crashed down on her; she welcomed the gush of water into the kettle and the incremental roar of its boiling. Step by step, she continued getting through the day. Processing would come later; that particular Pending tray was already overflowing. Right now, coping moment to moment had to suffice.

10

Visitor

The garden held its breath with a stillness beyond the lack of any breeze; the air grey with a heaviness, a non-visual colour which had nothing to do with the impending summer rain. Bethany looked around from her seat at the well-used metal table, its finely wrought detail flecked with tiny spots of rust and stubborn traces of bird droppings. A memory sparked to unexpected life; her father making her primary school self shriek with laughter as he mock-threatened to replace the worn old toothbrush he used for cleaning those hard to reach traces with her own. She saw him clearly in her mind, waving from the sunlit past of summer afternoons; the old brush in one hand and her pink-handled junior one in the other as though conducting an orchestra, pretending to get them mixed up and lowering hers towards the table. Her mother laughed in the doorway even as she shook her head and muttered something about not encouraging toilet humour.

 A wave of melancholy swept over the adult Bethany as the memory faded, superseded by the hiatus of this sorrow-charged evening. This was life after Gerry Sawyer; the plants and lawn he tended continuing inexorably without him. Today, everything natural and free radiated an unfamiliar pause; a respectful waiting for some formal cue that it was fitting to resume. Bethany's eyes shimmered with an acute empathy; suspended in loss, her own need for clarity and a recognisable route map through this strange new time clamouring its internalised shame against the requisite calm.

The sound of a car approaching infused gradually into the quiet street, calling Bethany's attention as it stopped at the gate. The beige Cambusmenzie Taxis logo shocked her mind back to that place from several days ago; gripping the edge of the table, she quickly forced the memory into fast forward, replacing those images with Diane, Farolita and Des. Jellied eels slithered comically into her hastily reframed mental landscape, threatening an inappropriate burst of laughter. That would not do either! Focus; concentrate on what needs attention now.

That being the compact woman getting out of the taxi, whose lively short bobbed hair, a shade somewhere between magenta and red, and tiny silver stud in her snub nose contrasted with her sober dark grey jacket and navy dress.

"Emma!"

Bethany scarcely registered the ugly scrape of the chair as she pushed it back and the grating rattle of metal legs on the patio as she bumped the table; the perennial background despair at her spatial judgement suppressed for once by the bright, unexpected arrival of her cousin from London.

"I called your mum; she said it was OK to pop round and see you both for a bit ahead of tomorrow. How are you doing? Oh, Beth. I am so sorry."

Returning her cousin's hug, Bethany searched her mind for a reference to Emma visiting. Had her mother understandably forgotten to mention it, or had she failed to retain the conversation? Oh well, another uncertainty to shoulder; she filed it neatly away in the usual vault as she stepped back to take in this up to date version of the cousin whom she had not seen in person for several years.

"Of course it's OK; I'm so happy to see you. I know it's not supposed to be anything other than a sad time, but I've been looking forward to seeing you as one of the positives of the day and it kind of makes me feel a bit closer to Dad again too. I know you were in touch quite a lot recently;

Mum said one of your housemates is getting into a new line of work in architecture and Dad had been giving her advice?"

"Yes, that's right. Ivanna. She's been so thankful for your dad's input. Look, I know this isn't the time to talk about it but I feel I should tell you; although I know there had been a rift between you over the past year, your dad loved you very much, right to the end. I don't know the details and it's none of my business, but I know he did regret some of the things he said to you. He didn't know how to approach you to put it right, but he did feel it."

"Thanks, Em; that truly means a lot. How's Blair? I'm sorry they couldn't get time off work; I know they'd have wanted to be here."

"They're keeping well, thanks, and yes, they would have loved to have been here. To see their own family as well as to pay respects tomorrow. Unfortunately a partner's uncle isn't considered a close enough relative for them to get leave, and they had no annual leave left. We can video call them once we've seen your mum."

"Gosh, look at me thoughtlessly keeping you out here. Of course; let's go in. I was only out for a bit of fresh air anyway"; she was gabbling again, mortified at having selfishly monopolised her cousin's time. Shaking her head and silently telling herself to do better, Bethany escorted Emma into the mourning hush of the house.

Tea cups and dainty cupcakes cleared away, Bethany joined Emma on the couch as Sheila excused herself to lie down for a while. The video call connected and Blair Dunsmuir appeared on the screen; their cropped, bleached white hair feathered sideways and forwards around their face, a slick of mauve lipstick offsetting the green cotton top of which a round neckline showed at the lower edge of the camera's view. Blair's fluid gender had been closer to masculine in the last photos Bethany had seen of them on

Sharon's social media pages; their hair slicked directly back and their shoulders squared beneath tartan shirts in a wide variety of hues over plain, neutral-coloured trousers. Always enthusiastic about their style, they had joked in the comments about their full wardrobe being the envy of many a boring cisgender icon. Bethany had wholeheartedly appreciated the joke and smiled to herself when a transgender friend of Blair and Emma's made a play on words involving closets which had occurred to her too; thankful to have worked out long ago that as a cisgender person, regardless of her being in another LGBTQIAP+ category, it was a subject not in her lane to make puns about however much she enjoyed wordplay.

"Hey! Bethany, I'm so sorry about your father. Ivanna's out right now and so is Aldo, but we've all set aside time tomorrow to have a moment and raise a glass to Gerry."

"Thanks, Blair; that's so thoughtful of you all, especially when you've such busy lives and Aldo doesn't know us. Seeing how many people are honouring my dad helps to ease the intensity here; it makes a difference knowing that we're not alone in this bubble."

"You're absolutely not alone. If there's anything Emma and I can do to help, you know where we are. We must keep in touch more; it shouldn't be up to you to reach out at a time like this. Gerry dying has made us both think, and we will make time."

Bethany nodded, swallowing a sudden treacherous lump in her throat; she thanked Blair and squeezed her cousin's shoulder as she went into the kitchen to wash the dishes and leave Emma to talk privately with her partner. She would not admit it to Emma, but the thought of their hectic schedules and shared living quarters flooded her with something close to panic. Would she find herself having to cope with communal living one day? The dark social and sensory shadow of future care needs lurked in wait over a secret, far-flung horizon in her brain; a landmark already looming proportionally closer as she neared her fifties, the death of a parent further enhanced those fears. It was a cruel double-edged sword; her real and valid future anxieties heightened at the same time as her own needs must be put completely aside and not spoken of in order to support her mother and respect that observed hierarchy of bereavement.

Was she a monster for feeling so keenly that being far enough up in that hierarchy to be hit hard by the loss but not right at the top had its own unique difficulties? The part of her which was growing in strength to self-advocate in order to put on her own oxygen mask and help others in turn sensibly interjected that the problem lay in society's insistence on making everyone's needs into a contest. Validation and support were lauded as some kind of exclusive prize to be won by an elite of fault-free suffering. Who the hell got to judge anyway? Ivanna was not a relative at all; she was a housemate of a seldom-seen cousin who had never met Gerald Sawyer in person. She was also someone who had fled war in her native country, rebuilt her life and forged a new career away from her first language and everything else familiar, to then suddenly lose a cherished mentor. Should anyone suggest to Bethany that Ivanna had any less right to grieve; to be visibly upset and experience difficult emotions as a result of the loss than she did, she knew exactly how she would react. Yet she struggled to feel allowed to make space for her own needs; to so much as acknowledge them in her own mind, let alone ask for help or a bit of moral support to address them.

These things needed to be spoken about. Break those taboos! But first, she needed to face burying her father. More immediately, she had to fix her camouflage and prepare to bid a coping, unselfish, undemanding goodbye to Emma as she took the luminous novelty of her presence back to an impersonal hotel in Falkirk, leaving that texture of greyness to blanket the house once more.

Emma called the local taxi firm and reported that there would be someone free in ten minutes to take her to her hotel. Bethany accepted her invitation to wait with her and they walked out to the gate, glad of the opportunity to breathe the evening air despite the lingering humidity.

"As Blair said, Beth, if there is anything we can do to help; please know that's not lip service, we have a fair idea of how alone you must be feeling. This may not be the most apt time to mention it, but as you know, Blair's family lives around this area and their Uncle Murray is a solicitor, in Stirling. He deals with matters around, well, preparing for the administration and responsibilities of dealing with the estate. He's done executorship for a couple of people Blair knows; at least one of whom is neurodivergent, and that person told Blair that their uncle was the most respectful, understanding and genuine professional he had ever dealt with. They said to me to mention it to you; though I'm wary as it feels disrespectful to Sheila, I also remember from when my father died how much it made us think about our mother's mortality. And there are three of us to support one another. Even though one of that three is Louise."

Bethany snorted a laugh at the affectionate but justifiable caveat. Her middle cousin had a different nature from Emma and Sharon's; Emma would be fully aware that Louise had a history of what could kindly be termed a complex relationship with her neurodivergent family members.

"Och, she's come a long way, but I know what you mean."

"I'm so glad you're not upset or offended. It's such a delicate time."

"Not at all; I appreciate that it took guts for you to raise this with me, and you're absolutely right. Especially with Mum's cancer scare being so recent and under monitoring. I don't mind admitting it to you, Emma; I'm terrified of the future, and I would be immensely grateful if you could put me in touch with Blair's uncle once the funeral is over with. Would he see me just to give a bit of guidance on what to expect? I'd pay for his time, of course. I mean, obviously I'm learning bits of it right now, but I'm not sure how much of it I'll retain especially in the circumstances, and it's bound to feel different again when I'm facing it on my own."

"Murray would definitely see you for a chat and so that you have a familiar face to call upon officially once you need to. And he wouldn't charge for an initial informal consultation; Blair knows that from the people they referred to him before. Would you like them to give him a bit of background; is it OK to tell him you're autistic?"

"Yes please, and yes! Thank you for asking, but it's important he knows that I might need a bit more time to process whatever he tells me and that my tone, expressions and suchlike may seem different from what people expect."

"He won't judge you, I promise that, but thanks for making your consent clear. I will let Blair know and they will get in touch with Murray. He's a lovely man; the kind you want in your corner. Blair is very close to him."

"Sounds ideal! Thank you so much, and please say thanks to Blair too."

"I will."

After a few more minutes spent in comfortable contemplation side by side in their thoughts, Emma's taxi arrived and Bethany tapped into her renewed strength to smile as she waved it off; a small scale letting go which called for a disproportionate amount of fortitude in the midst of this maelstrom of now.

11

Funeral

Tremulous light breaking through grey-white clouds made a watercolour painting of what would be Bethany's indelible memories of this day as the funeral car slowly followed the hearse along Cambusmenzie's High Street. The glacial pace at once soothed and agitated her; the steady sensory input offset by the wish for these loaded, unfamiliar moments to be over.

An older couple coming out of a charity shop halted and the man removed his hat as they passed; two teenage girls, absorbed in their phones, didn't notice the cortège at all. A woman in a pink dress placed a quieting hand on the shoulder of her excited son as a snatch of his chatter about a new gaming app filtered briefly into their suspended cocoon of formality. Her mother's breathing hitched momentarily, caught up in a private instance of some randomly sparked association in her mind; feeling intrusive, Bethany focused on the straight-backed posture of the driver's black-clad head and shoulders in front of her as the cars turned at walking pace through the gates of St John's Church.

Seeking the morale boost of familiar allies in the groups of mourners turning to look at the procession, she quickly spotted Sharon's pale blonde, almost white hair. Diane was with her, talking to the McGraths; Bethany and Sharon's Aunt Sandra and Uncle Dave and their family. George's sandy hair was beginning to recede now; he cut a kindly and dignified figure as he stood with one arm each around his wife Jessie and daughter Hannah, the woman and girl subdued in their neat black dresses, court shoes and tights. Joseph and his husband Barry stood close together in elegantly coordinated suits, nodding attentively though their eyes never left the nearby oak bench where little Jacob Delaney McGrath perched nervously in his tiny formal jacket and kilt.

"Your dad would have loved that"; Sheila blinked rapidly as she undid her seatbelt, the action reminding Bethany to do the same. "He didn't say much, as you know, but he really was proud when Joseph and Barry adopted that lovely wee boy."

Bethany smiled, her words not there in the moment. For what seemed like the hundredth time that day, she felt for the tight velvet scrunchie that held her hair soberly in place and hid as much as possible of the lingering traces of her trademark blue dye. Her unpredictable mind flashed forward to when this would all be over with and she could restore her appearance to the comfort of familiarity; horrified at herself for such a disrespectful thought, she forced her attention back to making as poised an exit as she could from the car and helping her mother.

The Reverend Charmaine Swann met them on the neatly swept driveway where a few stray leaves had since fallen to the early wind and rain, fortunately both now receded to watery calm. Bethany stepped back deferentially as the minister greeted her mother first, taking both of Sheila's hands in her own with a gentle "How are you?" which had nothing whatsoever to do with social ritual. Turning to Bethany, Reverend Swann's eyes shimmered with compassion as she leaned in to whisper "You're doing a great job supporting your mother". Unable to trust herself to speak, she nodded and swallowed a threatening lump in her throat, watching as the minister returned to the doorway whilst she and her mother got into place behind the pallbearers who shouldered her father's coffin.

Focusing on the steady beat of their shoes on the stone floor got Bethany through the long, weighty walk down the aisle as her mother gripped her arm and the evocative strains of 'Amazing Grace' played on the bagpipes swelled the already emotionally charged air. Her mind was still trying to process the knowledge that the body in which her father had lived, the form in which she had known him, lay inside the casket being borne ahead of them by men he barely knew if at all. If they were local, he may have queued next to them in the post office, or exchanged comments in the club about a horse race, a by-election or that good old British topic, the weather. Now here they were carrying him to his eternal resting place. Her jaw ached with the need to be strong for her mother; to be seen to do it well enough to appease the wider family. She glimpsed Ginty Flett in a pew near the front, lace handkerchief ready to mop veiled eyes which regarded Bethany narrowly as if daring her to let her 'difficulties' show today. Fighting the urge to look around for Sharon and Diane, she resolutely faced forward, guiding her mother to their seats as the pallbearers gently set her father down.

Reverend Swann spoke with respect, empathy and a little quiet humour. The hymns and prayers passed in a haze of unreality amid Bethany's frantic attempts to make her shaking fingers find the right pages quickly enough for both her mother and herself; every fumble sounding like shearing metal to her panicked ears. Then the pallbearers were taking up their positions once more and it was time to finally lay Gerald Sawyer to rest in the hallowed ground.

The casket seemed a long way down; deeper than Bethany's imagination or preparation had led her to expect. The petrichor smell of the damp soil, normally a fresh and comforting natural scent, felt infused with a hint of the closed-in mustiness of the church. She was nearer to the edge than she would have preferred, though well within a safe margin as she supported her trembling mother to throw in the symbolic handfuls of earth. The burial was over in minutes, but her physical and emotional reactions would have to be held in check for a while yet as she thankfully returned to the path.

The pale sun was attempting another comeback as the mourners emerged once more into freedom to talk and share. As a shaft of sunlight fell across the traces of soil around the freshly dug grave, the implications seemed to hit home for little Jacob, who began to cry.

"I don't want worms to eat Uncle Gerry!"

As Joseph and Barry hastened to comfort their son, Sheila's older sister Carole turned to Sandra with a disapproving look; Bethany caught something about "surely they prepared him" and "in front of poor Sheila". Mindful of her responsibility being first and foremost to her mother, she was relieved to hear Sandra step up for the distressed boy.

"Of course they prepared him, but all it takes is another kid to say something, perhaps at one of the play groups. No amount of preparation could have stopped this from being scary and upsetting for him, because he is a little child, Carole, and so are his peers. He knows not to directly ask any questions of Sheila or Bethany, but you cannot expect a five-year-old to master the nuances of giving people space in an environment like this!"

As Aunt Carole came over to embrace her bereft sister, Bethany took the opportunity to go to reassure the little boy. Joseph was cradling him, reminding him that Uncle Gerry was no longer in the shell they had just symbolically buried; that he was free, living on in all of their hearts and minds, and that his body was going back to Nature but did not contain Gerry the person, any more than a house he had moved out of.

"Worms are a part of Nature, anyway", he was saying, "just like the bees; remember Daddy Barry telling you about how important those are? Worms are slimy and bees can sting!"; the little boy giggled at his playful tone; "but we need them; we need all of Nature, and it's a good thing that what were our bodies can go back to that once we don't need them any more. You loved feeling the soil going through your fingers when we were helping Granddad Dave in the garden. It all feels different and sad today, I know, but we're all a part of that gorgeous big picture."

Bethany stood still, mesmerised by her cousin's beautiful words and the space he and Barry had created for Jacob to be allowed to be a child, not a miniature adult. Joseph looked up as he registered her presence.

"Bethany! I am so…"

"Please, Joseph, don't apologise. What you just said to this precious wee boy is as meaningful a tribute to my dad as any eulogy or service. All stages of life should be respected here. Hey, Jacob, you have done so well getting all dressed up and being with the grown-ups doing and seeing things you've never had to before when everybody is being sad and serious." She crouched down closer to his height, his wide eyes dry again as he looked at her with fascination. "Thank you for being here today; it's lovely to see you, and you look fabulous!"

Jacob pointed over towards the grave, his attention caught by something colourful. Bethany looked in the direction of his small finger; a tortoiseshell butterfly swooped down and alighted on a nearby gravestone, its wings spread to the meagre sun filtering through the trees.

"Saint ass!"

At least, that was what it sounded as though he said as he turned to point towards the church. Bethany hurriedly stifled a burst of much needed if inappropriate mirth; Jacob swung his arm back round to point to the butterfly again, and the penny dropped.

"Did you say 'stained glass'? Like the windows in the church?"

The child nodded enthusiastically.

"Well, you know, now that you mention it, you're right! The butterfly's wings do look just like a stained glass window. A tiny portal into the colourful world of the little things around us. What a lovely thought to have and to share with us, Jacob; thank you. I will always remember that."

Tears shone in Bethany's eyes as she stood up and looked at her grateful cousin, his own eyes brimming with emotion. A memory flashed into her mind of a Christmas Day long ago when the toddler who would become this caring father gazed wide-eyed in fascination at the metallic swirl of a hanging festive decoration; the two of them watching it as it spun in an alcove away from the hectic family dinner table, catching the draught and dazzle of the overwhelmingly busy home.

Barry, who had been reassuring a concerned Sandra and Dave, returned to his husband's side; the two men hugged Bethany then linked arms and reached out their free hands to their son. She looked around for her mother, suddenly fearful that she had neglected her for too long; to her relief, Sheila was deep in conversation with Louise, and her husband Nev. Which brought Bethany to another hoped-for reunion as Louise's daughter rushed over to her.

"Lucy!"

Bethany embraced the young woman to whom she had become an effective mentor over the years as their shared experiences of being neurodivergent bonded them. They did not get to meet in person quite so often now that Lucy divided her year between university terms in Edinburgh and vacations in Caithness, to where her mother and stepfather had moved in order to take up a business opportunity.

"Oh, Beth. Today must be so hard, in so many ways. How's it really going?"

"Well, it's going."

Lucy smiled in understanding, realising that Bethany needed to keep her camouflage skills intact for the time being.

"I'm staying at Charlene's for a few nights; Mum and Nev are driving home later, they'll stop off in Inverness overnight to break up the journey but I wanted to catch up properly with Shaz and everybody in Inverbrudock. I'll be getting the train back up. Charlene is so sorry she couldn't make it; Brandon had an appointment that couldn't be rescheduled."

It was Bethany's turn to nod in understanding. She too was close to Charlene and Brandon; the siblings who lived in the other half of the house, originally one single property, next door to where her Aunt Carole and Uncle Hector had raised Sharon, Louise and Emma. Aunt Carole's home had been the scene of those childhood Christmas gatherings.

"Anyway", Lucy was saying, "I hoped I would get the chance of a quick word with you, to give you Charlene and Brandon's apologies and condolences in person."

Bethany and Lucy walked over to where Sheila was in conversation with Carole, and Reverend Swann who was holding a spray of assorted roses.

"Ah, there you are, Bethany. I said to Sheila, would you like to take a rose and put it in with your father before everyone makes their way over the road for some tea and sandwiches? Your mother wants a red one; she said that you might like a yellow one, that yellow flowers are your favourite."

"That's a lovely idea! Thank you. Yes, I'd love a yellow one, please."

This was it; this was her chance to do the one last thing she needed to in order to make her peace.

"Actually, Reverend Swann, er, please may I have a white one too? Mum's right; yellow is my favourite. But…"

Carole drew in a sharp breath beside her, catching her eye and giving a small but distinct shake of her head with a warning glare. Did she honestly think Bethany was going to mention the real reason out loud?

"Dad had family in Yorkshire; I know he enjoyed his trips there as a boy. I think he would like a white rose in there too."

"Of course!"; the minister took out the three roses, setting down the rest of the bouquet on the bench and handing the red one to Sheila, who walked over and dropped it into the grave, murmuring something privately for herself and her husband. After a respectful pause, the minister handed the remaining two roses to Bethany: "Careful of the thorns, dear".

No such warning had been given to Sheila; hierarchically the most bereft, the most likely distracted, but without that nebulous Something that caused autistic people to be seen as more likely to mess up and be clumsy, regardless of whether they had disclosed their neurodivergence. All roses had thorns. Another microaggression; another paper cut to the soul, in a situation where to defend herself would be an enormous faux pas. Another reminder of a time when Bethany had longed to be out of all this crap for good. Even at her own father's graveside she could not be allowed equal standing.

It stung.

She choked back the bitter frustration and carried on.

"For all of the father you were, Dad."

She dropped the roses into the grave and stepped away, gasping with shock at her Aunt Carole stood so close by that she must have heard that private tribute.

"Yorkshire, hmm?"

"Yes, the white rose is the emblem of…"

"Do not get smart with me. I know fine well what that was about, and I need to be sure you will not be so selfish as to indulge that today and upset your mother."

Bethany could feel it coming; the darkness, the shutdown of situational mutism when she most needed to speak her truth. Why would Carole think that of her and attack her, being the one to create a potential scene, not to mention eavesdropping on her private moment with her father when she had already come up with a perfectly good cover? Startling her near the open graveside too! How was that acceptable; why didn't someone tell *her* 'Careful'? How come *she* wasn't getting criticised for actually doing something reckless, when Bethany was warned before taking hold of a couple of flowers? Rage surged within as the constantly, unfairly, pre-emptively chastised child she had been began to take over; less predominant now since Bethany had found a good balance in her life and had supportive people around her, but always there and stronger than her overwrought emotions could repress at a time like this. She shocked herself with her thoughts, imagining throwing Aunt Carole into the open grave. How *dare* she?

Then the miracle happened; Sharon was there, ushering Carole away.

"Mother! What the hell?", her cousin hissed furiously. "That was a beautiful gesture, extremely *well thought out*, and it was a private moment for Bethany! You are out of order!"

Bethany cast a final glance down at the three roses lying on top of the coffin and silently prayed that her father was not looking upon her with anger from wherever he was. She hoped with all of her being that he had found the peace he never knew in life after their greatest loss; the real reason she cast an extra flower into his grave.

Forcing her thoughts back to Jacob and his stained glass window butterfly, Bethany turned from the void and the injustice and walked on unsteady legs to escort her mother to the buffet.

12

Wake

The function room at Cambusmenzie Golf Club had no natural light and a heavily patterned carpet which dragged Bethany's eyes on an unwanted tour. All that was missing from the typical social gathering sensory assault was the loud music; she silently gave thanks that she would not have to deal with that. Her mother had declined her offer to fix her a plate from the sandwich buffet and gone to speak with some relatives on her father's side. She hauled her gaze away from the chaos underfoot to look at her father's photograph propped up in its frame on a black cloth where the DJ's booth was normally set up. Gerald Sawyer had cut a handsome figure in his dinner jacket; his dark hair greying at the temples, more so recently than it had been when the photo had been taken. His face was rounded enough to give him a look of jollity, tempering the keen observant glint of his blue-grey eyes. She instinctively checked the tidiness of her own hair yet again. Sharon and Diane hurried over to her.

"Beth, are you OK? I am so sorry about what my mother did to you. It was a beautiful gesture with the extra rose; I have to admit I was completely gone at that and you have Diane to thank for spotting that my mum had followed you over to the grave, and clocking her body language."

"Thank you; both of you. I get that she's being a protective big sister. But I'd already come up with a suitable way to get around mentioning anything sensitive; I don't get why she was so angry with me. I'm fifty next year and I'm still that child who can't be trusted, despite being in the act of proving that I can be tactful and aware of other people's feelings!"

"You were never a child who couldn't be trusted. And even if Sheila knew fine well why you really wanted to put that extra rose in there, which she probably did; it's bound to have been in her mind today, I'm sure she would be glad you did it and in such a thoughtful way."

"Sharon is right"; Carole's voice broke in softly from behind them. "Bethany, I owe you an apology. I was being overprotective of my sister; she doesn't talk about…"

Diane placed a brief, gentle hand on Bethany's arm and nodded respectfully to Carole as she excused herself; "This is a moment for the family; I'll be over there catching up with Lucy."

"You are family, Di, but thank you"; Bethany watched her best friend walk away, the glare of the fluorescent lights falling soft on her platinum blonde hair.

"I'm glad you found a good friend there", Carole was saying. "I have heard that she gave a lot of support to Lucy when she was struggling last year. Your mother was talking to me about her loss which she never normally speaks of, before the funeral and it made me overly vigilant. I didn't take in the fact that you had already recognised and demonstrated the need to be sensitive. If I'm completely honest, I don't think you should have done it; I think you should have found a way which entirely spared your mother. Did you imagine it wouldn't occur to her; that she wouldn't already be thinking about it? I do feel it was a bit self-indulgent…"

"Nice apology, Mum", muttered Sharon through clenched teeth. "Already morphing into another attack on her!"

"But I should not have interfered with your last farewell to your father. I ought to have had more consideration for what you are processing as well as Sheila."

"Fair enough, Aunt Carole; you are entitled to your opinion and I respect that, but I stand by what I did and how I did it. As you have pointed out yourself, I wouldn't have been reminding my mother of anything she wasn't thinking about already. I appreciate your support of her though, and thank you for your kind words about Diane too. You have said your piece and I hear you, but I think it would be best if you could give me some space for the rest of today, please. I need to focus on my own psychological safety if I am to properly support my mother."

Carole gave a tight nod and turned on her heel, making her way over to Louise and Nev.

"Phew"; Sharon shook her head and pretended to mop her brow. "That was so uncalled-for. She may be entitled to her opinion as you graciously said, but this was not the time or the place for anything other than a heartfelt apology after what happened at the graveside. You handled yourself brilliantly."

"Thanks, Shaz. Though I shouldn't take any credit given the thoughts I was having at the time. They were not gracious."

"Not gracious? I know she's my mum, but had I been in your shoes I would have been imagining pushing her into the grave!"; Sharon's eyes widened and she clapped a hand to her mouth. "God, that's really inappropriate; sorry!"

Bethany hastily suppressed both a loud laugh and the impulse to confess.

"You'd be surprised. I'm working on my reactivity, and I can see a difference, but the internal frustration is as strong as ever. I'm talking 'Event Horizon' levels of violent inner darkness. Now who's being inappropriate, bringing up a film like that at a funeral! But even here I cannot get a break from the constant drip drip drip of 'thin slice judgements'. I must look up the article I read about those on the NeuroClastic website; it's the best summing up I've seen of how and why we get doubted based on some vibe we apparently give off. Besides your mum's contribution, I got yet another singling out; being told to be careful of the thorns on the roses when my mother wasn't given any warning with hers. The minister of all people, who had told me I was doing well!"

"Which you are, and the warning doesn't cancel that out, though I know it feels that way to you and I understand why. And I'm sorry that happened today. But it may have been something as simple as you having two roses to handle when your mum had one. Or, if you flip it, rather than it being a case of assuming you're less capable, perhaps she was subconsciously thinking of you having an extra load to cope with today with the social and sensory demands and that she was wanting to spare you having to think of absolutely everything."

" Trying To Be Nice! I know, I'm a horrible…"

"No! I don't mean that; I'm not diminishing how you feel. I get that the issue is that she said it to you but not Sheila; she could have said it to both of you. I get how it feels infantilising. I just wish I could take away some of the pain it causes you; that's why I'm suggesting a different context and motivation, not to say you're wrong to feel the way you do but to try and separate out the instances where it's not about judging you or making assumptions about your capabilities. What I'm getting at is, to the minister, it may have been a gesture to convey to you that you deserve a bit of extra kindness and support; it likely never entered her head that you would feel criticised or belittled by it. She doesn't know your very real reasons for finding it hurtful."

"I know; I get what you mean. There's a part of me that thinks it was a subconscious choice that I would need the warning and not my mum because her rose was a romantic red one for her relationship with her husband, which elevates her above needing warnings. I know that shouldn't bother me as an aromantic asexual, but on principle it does."

"That's down to our society's conditioning to elevate sex and romance above all else. Aroace or not, we all get that hierarchy forced upon us."

"Yes; it adds to the feelings of othering, even when it comes from people who have no way of knowing anything about my relationship status. You're probably right; it was most likely because I had two and my mum had one. It's always going to be raw for me though. The singling out itself, and the refusal to try to understand where I'm coming from. I can laugh at the warnings on, for instance, tins of salmon which say 'contains fish'. It puts it in perspective in a way; it's an example of how far litigation culture has become embedded into our collective consciousness. But it's not personal. It's not the same as if I were doing my food shopping and had a tin of salmon in my basket and everyone in front of me had the same tin, same size and brand, same wording on it. Imagine them all being served without comment and then when it came to me, the cashier saying slowly and loudly, 'now pet, this has *salmon* in it; if you're allergic to fishies, you can't have this!' This is the hill I will die on, Shaz; probably amid a cacophony of people telling me to watch I don't fall down it!"

"And your passionate advocating for autonomy is much needed; I will always support you in that. But you need a break from carrying that today."

"Yes, I do. Have you seen Emma? I haven't had the chance to speak to her yet, and I need to check on my mum too."

"Emma's over there with Mum and Louise and Nev; your mum was sitting with two other women, I think they're a couple from your dad's side of the family? Ah yes, there they are at the buffet."

Bethany followed Sharon's gaze towards the tables.

"Oh, wonderful. Yep; there they are, and I really ought to go and speak to them. Perfect Cousin Miriam and her wife."

Bo and Miriam Fanshawe carried themselves with the air of two sturdy trees grown together over decades; their entwined roots screened from outside view beneath the solid earth-mother practicality of their brisk, no-nonsense personalities. Neatly styled greying hair with lingering traces of chestnut and mahogany framed their alert, lightly made-up faces and skimmed the collars of their classic black suits. Bethany's mother sheltered in their shade, stoic yet visibly frail; her shoulders relaxed for the first time since before the funeral cars left the house. As Bethany approached, Sheila took a small step closer to Bo; Miriam came forward, appraising her cousin with guarded eyes.

"Bethany. We are both so sorry for your loss; such a difficult day for your mother and you."

The emphasis on 'your mother' was subtle but clear.

"Thank you for coming. You're both looking well."

"Right. Speaking of being well, your mother is going to need your support now. When are you going to be moving home?"

"I already live at home; that is in Perth. As is my job, my support service, and most of my friends are there or more reachable from there. You wouldn't expect me to move back to my *childhood* home if I had a partner. I will of course be phoning and visiting more often. It's not that far away."

"Well then, isn't it about time you thought about learning to drive? Autism is only a barrier if you choose to let it be one. Bo's nephew is on the spectrum and he's been driving for years."

The familiar comet of mixed irritation, exhaustion and adrenalin-spiked fear rocketed through Bethany, sporting a tail of poignant humour as she was reminded of Diane and their 'Minister's Cat' satire.

"First of all, unless it is the nephew's stated preference for how to refer to his autism, it sounds like prejudice when non-autistic people squeamishly use euphemisms like 'on the spectrum'. It undermines the point you're trying to make about autism, which is an ill-informed generalisation anyway. I have never once said, to you or anybody else, that I cannot drive because I am autistic. I am well aware that there are many autistic people who drive. Autism is more varied than you think. My reasons are more specific than that, but I'm not going to stand here breaking them down for you at my father's funeral."

"Your father was Sheila's husband! It's not all about you. It's time to step up and accept your responsibilities to your mother. And another thing, this quirk about contacting you by typed message and not phoning your mobile..."

Bethany held up her hand, palm outwards.

"Whoa. Hold the bus. Hold the *Megabus Gold*."

Raising her voice would get her shushed and rebuked for making a scene; leaning in for emphasis would bring accusations of aggression. Sweat broke out on Bethany's palms as her heart rate increased and her head began to throb.

"It is not a quirk. I have an issue with auditory processing and I cannot hear what people are saying on the phone if there is other noise going on. That is reality. It is not something I can turn off at will, however much the circumstances demand it. It is part of my profile of disability; however inconvenient, it is valid. Accommodating it is necessary for me to be able to do what I need to, not a favour or a special concession. If you were my employer you would be perilously close to breaking the law right now, calling a requested reasonable adjustment for accessibility 'a quirk'. As my cousin, well, you may not be breaking any laws but you're being wilfully ignorant and bigoted!"

Bethany glanced around to check for clear space behind her before stepping back, abruptly aware of her dry eyes aching from the prolonged contact she had forced them to make. Miriam's face was a picture of affronted perplexment.

"So what if your poor mother has another cancer scare and it's bad news this time? If she has to go into hospital and people need to phone you and you're not at home or work?"

"Then I won't be able to make out a word they're saying, Mim! That is a fact, no matter how important the call. By being clear about what I need in order to access the information they have to get across, I am doing what I can to make sure I am able to receive and respond to it more quickly. That is not 'making it about me'; it is making sure I am in a position to do my bit. What is it about that concept that people don't get? I don't want us to be enemies; I'm trying to communicate honestly and constructively here."

"It all seems like excuses to me, Bethany. Autism being a disability when it suits you. I mean, what's all that 'different not less' and Autistic Pride all about if it's such a problem?"

"Autism, as with other neurodivergences, is a disability in the sense that it qualifies for reasonable adjustments. Some autistic people don't consider themselves disabled; that depends on the individual's circumstances and is their choice, not to mention that it often means they have various privileges. Autistic Pride is not a universal status for all autistic people all of the time; it came out of a need to recognise the positive aspects and the contributions which we can make *given the right environment and any support we need*, which I've never denied. It should not be confused with autism being all sunshine and roses, nor should people infer from the existence of Autistic Pride that the difficulties we have are some form of optional add-on or can be overridden by willpower or anything else. And what exactly is your point about 'different not less'? Are you suggesting that 'proper' disabled people by your definition of the term, whatever the disability, *are* less? You need to do some reading up, big time. Bo too if she shares the appalling discriminatory views you've expressed today. Look up neurodivergent authors, not archaic outside viewpoints. Read Elle McNicoll; Chloé Hayden; Katherine May. Follow pages like 'Just Jeni'; she's based up in Aviemore, you would learn so much from a page like hers and other neurodivergent voices' social media accounts coming up in your feed. You shouldn't stop at white neurodivergents' writing either. Read the testimonies brought together by Marcia Brissett-Bailey and anything written or edited by Kala Allen Omeiza, for example, then check your privilege. I'll gladly email you a list of suggestions!"

"Is all this crusading more important than being there for your mother?"

"Crusading. Right. You know what; I'm done with hearing hateful rubbish today of all days. I can and will do both; show up for my fellow autistic people and for my mother, who in fact enjoys hearing about that part of my life. You clearly won't listen to me; perhaps you'll listen to her. Ask her about the work Diane and I are doing with my new boss! Meanwhile, I'm going to speak with her, I came over here to check in with her as well as to see you two."

"Yes, well. Try not to look too upset and watch what you say. You do tend to be clumsy and your tone can come across as abrasive. I know you can't help it with your condition…"

"Oho! So now I'm definitively autistic! My atypical facial expressions and my extra missteps as an undiagnosed neurodivergent child set in stone when it suits you; now who's picking and choosing my autistic traits and how much they count? You are out of line, Miriam. I am going to see my mother now, and then I need to check on my cousin Emma, who was close to Dad."

Bethany stepped around Miriam, who stood arms folded and glaring as she greeted Bo before exchanging some uncomfortable small talk about the buffet with her tired and distant mother. The weight of her paternal cousin's chastisement grated heavy as sandstone on her overwrought brain; fearful of giving Miriam any reason to feel proven right by running out of her internal resources with no opportunity to take time out to safely regroup, she queasily excused herself to seek out Emma. Hugging to herself the contraband relieved feeling at having a legitimate reason to get to safer company, she scurried past the rest of the buffet at which she had yet to show face. The sight of the food and cups reminded her to notice her dry mouth and tight throat. She poured water into a plastic cup, its texture perilously wobbly in her shaking hands; gulping half of it down, she quickly stifled a nervous burp. "Oops; sorry about that, Dad", she murmured to the benignly smiling photograph; a smile now forever consigned to history.

"…disappointed that she told Mum to back off. I mean, it's good that she's better at sticking up for herself these days, I'll grant her that. It's been a good example to you", Louise briefly interrupted her diatribe to nod towards Lucy; "but honestly, Nev, I'd have thought she would give it a rest today. When we were children, she was like a temperamental tap; nothing came out of her mouth for ages and then there'd be an outburst gushing indiscriminately. It was either a drought or a flood!"

Nev snorted a laugh into his almost empty cup, having the good grace to freeze guiltily when he looked towards the buffet with a refill in mind and caught sight of Bethany. Lucy, still comforting a visibly fragile Emma, glared at her mother and shook her head as her aunt's eyes filled with tears.

"Will you two pack it in? It's her father's funeral for God's sake!", Emma hissed.

"Yes; you sound like a pair of school bullies. You're upsetting Emma, making me ashamed and look, Bethany's coming over!", added Lucy.

Bethany smiled tightly at an abashed Louise, who held up a conciliatory hand; "Sorry, Beth. I got carried away there because you hurt Mum's feelings."

"Right, well, there was a context to my asking her to give me space; I don't know how much she told you but I'm certainly not going to stand here and elaborate right now so you'll need to take my word for it. I appreciate you coming all this way; it's a long drive for you and I hope that what you take away from today is all fond memories of my dad."

Louise nodded, a faint tinge of embarrassment showing through her carefully applied make-up. "Yes, thank you, Bethany; Gerry was a wonderful man. Speaking of the long drive, we will have to leave fairly soon; we're dropping Lucy off in Inverbrudock."

"I'll keep an eye on Emma", Bethany assured Lucy as she hugged her tightly; "and I'll see you soon. Give my love to Charlene and Brandon, and lots of pets to Cheminot too"; the thought of their friends' big affectionate ginger cat brought an unexpected lump to her throat.

"How are you holding up, Em?"

Her cousin's dutifully forced smile was belied by the subtle tell as she unconsciously touched the side of her nose where the silver stud normally nestled. Originally intended to draw people's attention away from a faded scar; the legacy of a rollerblading fall, above the eyebrow on the opposite side of her face, it was as much a part of Emma now as anything with which she had been born.

"Oh, your stud; come on, you've done your bit by the older generation and kept it out in the church and at the burial. Have you got your compact mirror there? Let's go over there where it's quiet and I'll hold it while you put the stud back in. My dad may have been traditional and he'd have appreciated your gesture but he wouldn't want you feeling uncomfortable."

"Thank you, Beth. Mind you, I'm not sure how *my* dad would have felt about me having it in at all today!" Hector

Penhaligon had died several years earlier; he loomed large in many of Bethany's excruciating awkward-child memories. Only a rare showing of empathy from Carole had persuaded him to accept the sixteen-year-old Emma's pleas to allow her to have the piercing done. Bethany screened her cousin from the knots of people milling about, standing with her back to the room as she held the compact mirror for as long as it took for Emma's trembling hands to retrieve the stud from her clutch bag and fix it back into place.

"Better?"

"Yeah, much. You're a star, Beth, thinking of this when it's such a sad day for you. When I look back, you've had a lot to cope with on your own. I know Sharon's always had your back but it's not the same when you don't have peer support around you on a day-to-day basis. I wish I'd taken more time to get to know you when we were all at our family homes."

"It's natural to be focused on the immediate world around us when we're young; I was the same. Funerals make people think about their regrets too, but they're also a reminder that we're still here and we can choose our own paths. Social media presence is a blessing in that it helps people keep in contact on a more ongoing basis nowadays; it has its drawbacks and its detractors, but I always say as long as it works for you and not you for it, overall it's a positive. I wouldn't be without it, on my own terms. Anyway, I'd better see how my mum is doing, though when I last saw her she was in way more capable hands than mine"; Bethany raised her eyebrows in a 'message you the details later' kind of way as her mind replayed the highlights of her conversation with Miriam.

"Bethany!"; right on cue, Bo's clipped tones carried stridently across the room, closely followed by her person. "*There* you are. She's over here, Mim, talking to the lady with the *vivid* hair."

Cringing at the rudeness, Bethany gave Emma an apologetic look, receiving one of dawning understanding in return.

"Wild Cherry, actually, Bo; my dad always admired it on her, said the shade suited her. This is Emma Penhaligon; my aunt Carole's youngest daughter who has come from London to be with us all today. Emma; this is Bo Fanshawe, my cousin Miriam's wife. Miriam is a cousin on Dad's side."

Sparsely acknowledging Emma with the most cursory of nods, Bo curtly informed Bethany that Sheila would be coming to stay with her and Miriam for a few days, so that they could be sure she was all right. Refusing to rise to the bait, Bethany politely smiled and thanked her; the older woman turned away with one final disapproving glance at Emma's hair.

"God, I'm so sorry about that; how crass! Your hair is perfectly appropriate and Dad did love the colour."

"Hey, don't worry about it. When you said 'Wild Cherry', I think she thought it was my stage name!"

The cousins dissolved into peals of smothered laughter as Bethany once again compulsively checked the neatness of her own hair, hoping that letting her own blue dye fade had not made Emma feel self-conscious about keeping her colour. Red, she told herself, even with a pink tone, was closer to a natural colour than her deep blue. Oh, the complications of all these social nuances; worrying so much about keeping everybody happy was exhausting. Once again she reminded herself that it was impossible to avoid all potential conflict of interest in every meticulously thought out decision she made. Was it any wonder that so many neurodivergent and social anxiety-prone people had permanent fatigue issues?

She steered her mind to fully notice that Emma was laughing; that she had seen the funny side of Bo's impolite remark and that she had already been feeling better because

Bethany had helped her by enabling her to put her nose stud back in. Taking a deep breath, she forced herself to focus on the room and away from her gathering storm of frantic thoughts.

"She was a ray of sunshine, wasn't she?"; Emma shook her head, still amused. "I shouldn't say that; I don't know her, and she does seem to genuinely care about Sheila."

"Yes, she does; I'll always give her and Miriam credit where it's due, they do make an effort and keep in contact and they have been a big help to Mum especially when she had her cancer scare. Which is all that matters, especially today; that they're looking out for her."

"Well, that is important, but it's not all that matters, Beth. We all need to be looking out for you too. I get that the two of them will be grieving, but it hasn't stopped them from being kind to Sheila; there's no reason for it to create a barrier against also supporting you."

"Oh, that wasn't anything new or funeral related, Em! My relationship with those two has always been one of shotgun humility. I have never disputed that they have practical skills I don't, nor how important those are; I give them credit however much it rubs in how inadequate I'm feeling. They, on the other hand, never let me forget it"; she glanced around quickly to make sure she was not being overheard; "I've had years of it. 'Since *Bethany* can't *drive*'; 'Poor Sheila having to make allowances for her grown-up daughter's autism and not having any other, *normal* children to turn to'; 'Well, my wife and I have been making casseroles for thirty years because we are so *involved* in family and community life, we'd struggle to adjust to *cooking in a microwave* just for ourselves, ha ha!' All actual examples."

"Good God! 'Any normal children to turn to'? Bethany, that's vile! Practically eugenics apologism. How have we gotten to a state where somebody saying a thing like that barely registers as unacceptable?"

"Yes, you're right; it's depressingly unremarkable. Mind you, the casserole comment; I heard Dad say to Uncle Ray, 'Goodness, I feel old; did she say they made their first of these things thirty years ago?', and Ray said 'I think this is one of them!' I'm sure he was wisecracking and didn't mean it; I have to acknowledge they are good cooks. It was hilarious though!"

"Ha ha, good on your Uncle Ray! I wish that side of your family would give you as much grace and credit and fair-mindedness as you do them."

"I must admit, so do I. And I'm not claiming I can't cook either. I've never had the incentive to learn; Bo and Miriam do have a point about it being more feasible for that skill to develop when their lifestyle is more communal. It *is* more fiddly and less logical doing it for one, unless someone is specifically interested in it as in any other hobby. Not having followed a path that led me to learn something isn't the same as not being able to, and I've never assumed that on account of my autism. My not driving is different; I do have reasons, to do with coordination, concentration and perception, to believe that I would not be able to do it safely and I have chosen not to risk pursuing that. I realise that it's an unexplored unknown and I may be mistaken, but yes; I made a deliberate decision there based on my knowledge of myself as a whole, not any assumption about my neurotype. This view of my more solitary lifestyle as being a negative thing, though, and that their way of living is the only way; that is where I do have an issue. I can help people and contribute to the world in other ways. It's only been in the last year or so that I've come to recognise that they count."

"I'm glad you realise that. You know, Uncle Gerry truly adored you and was proud of you. He was always the type to say that about people more easily than he could say it to them, but it's true. I hope you can hold on to that."

"Thanks, Em, and he thought the world of you too."

Sharon waved at Bethany from across the room, evidently trying to get her attention; Emma indicated wryly that she was going to take her chances with the hair dye police and go to speak with Sheila as more people began to say their goodbyes and the crowd finally thinned out in the suddenly tired and desolate function room. Sheila was, to Bethany's relief, in fact in the less fiercely guarded company of her younger sister; Sandra and Dave McGrath were also getting ready to take their leave of her under Bo and Miriam's watchful eyes. Motioning to Sharon to give her a moment, Bethany relaxed into their circle of warm concern, taken back momentarily to that childhood feeling of allyship which had always come from her youngest aunt and uncle at family gatherings; a bridge between her out of her depth self and the rest of the adults. As Sandra and Dave went to rescue Emma, Bethany searched the room once more for the lighthouse of Sharon in the ebbing tide of familial faces.

13

Number 2 Baker Street

"Thank you so much!"; Sharon gave the thumbs up sign as she ended her call to the helpful receptionist at Stirling's Golden Lion Hotel. "They're happy to keep our bags for an extra couple of hours, Di."

"Are there delays on your trains home?", a concerned Emma asked as she returned from saying her farewells to the McGraths.

"No; as Aunt Sheila is going to stay with the Fanshawes for a few days, we're taking Bethany to the pub! I know you're staying in Falkirk again tonight, Em; are you up for a quick detour to Stirling?"

The stagnant droop of humidity finally lost its weary hold on the rain as they passed through the ticket gates at Stirling Station. A proactive railway employee in their high-viz jacket was already setting out the yellow wet floor warning signs as the four women crossed the concourse. Under the broad awning, they pulled up hoods and unfolded umbrellas, bracing themselves to dash through the torrent as it hurled itself from leaden skies to flare its last in liquid pewter starbursts around their feet. Shrieking at the sensory onslaught of the weather combined with release from the day's long-dreaded formalities, they crossed the busy interchange and then Murray Place. They laughingly encouraged one another up the wide sweep of Friars Street to its junction with Baker Street and the panoramic, fairy-lit allure of the pub on the corner.

Number 2 Baker Street called itself precisely as and where it was. The light cream painted brickwork showed original wooden beams to their maximum, timeless effect; contrasting stretches of broad panelling in dark and neutral colours offset the urban streetwise glow of starkly fitted, bright incandescent bulb lights. A multitude of dainty, warm white LED strings lit an invitation outside and a welcome inside, softened to a blended haze by the steam of life swirling in from a thorough Scottish downpour. The foursome found a table at the back which allowed an equal view of the rain-blurred cityscape and the neatly organised bar.

"I could never come in here, especially on a day like this, without half expecting Gerry Rafferty to walk in and that saxophone riff start up!", smiled Diane as she folded her coat over the back of a chair and shook out her blonde hair. "I mean, obviously I know the song is referring to Baker Street in London, but there's something about city rain and saxophone music."

"Yes, I get exactly what you mean"; Bethany looked around, taking in details new to her as she saw the familiar pub through the lens of Diane's complicated memories of Stirling. "I'm glad you feel comfortable coming back here now."

"Thanks, Beth. It means a lot that you're thinking of that today. Yeah, I'm at peace with having cut ties with most of the family now; I have a baseline of contact with my sister, nothing too complicated and as for the rest of them, they're strangers now. I wish them well and hope they learn in time not to be ableist bigots, for the sake of future generations, but I don't miss them. It's funny; that song, with its message about realising where you need to be in life and making peace with that, feels more meaningful than ever here now aside from the coincidence of the title. In my case, it's a realignment rather than leaving one scenario for the other. My life is in Inverbrudock, but I also get to reclaim my roots in Stirling. My parents are moving to the Borders to be nearer to their beloved son and his respectable capitalism.

It's all good; it is a bit of security and a support network for them all and I'm happy for them. And I get to come to Stirling again without being so on edge. Win win!"; she saluted the others with the chunky textured whisky glass handed to her by Sharon. "Anyway, Beth, today is about you, and the only Gerry we should be focused on is your dad. Seriously, well done for how you handled yourself today."

Bethany quickly brushed away a tear, self-consciously extending the movement to fix a strand of hair which had escaped from its clip when a spoke of her umbrella glanced off it in the rush to get it folded down and put away once indoors.

"Thank you, and to all of you for being there supporting me. I appreciate it more than I know how to express"; she took a shaky breath and a hearty swig of her drink. "I know that today is only the start. Between the gravitas of the occasion and the input of the likes of Ginty Flett and Bo and Miriam, I am all too well aware that my mother could have another cancer scare at any time. The day is going to come when I have to go through all of this again, but without there being a remaining parent to team up with, and there will be a house to deal with. I know this sounds selfish, disrespectful, and that I should have the decency to wait until after today before talking about it, but I'm scared!"

Beside her, Emma gently squeezed her left hand; Sharon and Diane focused intently across the table, holding space, their body language standing in for touch and leaving her drinking arm free movement. This was her family.

"It is absolutely not selfish", Sharon said firmly. "You have every right to be scared and to need to reach out about it. Anyone putting pressure on you about the future as you're going through this needs to have a word with themselves. It feels to some people like their way to contribute, making all these self-righteous proclamations, but it's not constructive. You are not on your own with this.

If and when the time comes that Sheila needs support, or when you have to face losing her, you must hold on to the fact that being next of kin doesn't mean you have to do it all alone. There are things other people can help with, and you have all of us around and behind you lifting you up for the things you will need to do. You are allowed to gravitate away from the people who bluster, judge and order you around and go towards the people who are kind and supportive and build you up. In fact, it's more than allowed; it's essential."

"Sharon's right", asserted Emma with another subtle squeeze of Bethany's hand. "And when it comes to legal advice and guidance on the practical matters, remember that Blair's Uncle Murray will help you with confirmation even if he's retired by then and the advice is informal. Blair's dad has contacts in the estate agent business too, who will be able to help you with the house. The brothers have worked together to help bereaved clients before; they have built up working relationships with house clearance firms too, so they can take a lot of the load off. Murray always says that it's important to him to remind himself with each new client that what is a normal day's work for him is huge, new, scary and exhausting for them."

"Yes, he sounds like a lovely person. That is the kind of attitude I'll need; that every bereaved person dealing with estate affairs needs! It feels right now as though this upheaval and chaos will never end; as though nothing will ever settle into routine again. I've been going between my own flat and my mum's house regularly for years now, yet I'm suddenly getting caught out by everything in a way I never have before. When I'm in one home, I'll go to where things are kept in the other. I'll go to switch the kettle on at the bit where the switch is on the one at the other place. Mine's got it in the top of the handle; Mum's has it near the base. And don't get me started on the taps. That's two examples out of many. I always used to adapt more easily;

I didn't have to think about it so much, but now my muscle memory is deserting me. Then there's the cumulative frustration when it keeps happening. The guilt, too; I'm supposed to up my game, not get worse! My executive functioning is a disgrace right when my mum needs it bolstered for her to lean on. It was already taking a hit more than usual because I'm entering menopause. I don't need all this pressure on top of grieving for my dad!"

"What you're describing there is all entirely natural", soothed Sharon, "while at the same time, your frustration is absolutely valid. You raise an extremely important point about menopause. That's a tough transition of its own and the age ranges involved mean that a lot of people who go through menopause will experience a parent bereavement during that time; quite possibly without realising and being aware to make allowances if it begins during a time of bereavement because the effects will not be so noticeable when everything is so churned up already. Trouble concentrating; mood fluctuations; periods out of sync when they were regular before; memory lapses; skin changes; appetite and weight changes; so many issues which can be common to both and get attributed solely to the visible stress of the bereavement when in fact there could be other things happening in the body, such as the onset of menopause or perimenopause, which need their own acknowledgement, management and mitigations. It's not something anyone can willpower their way out of, and people need to understand that. There's no quick fix; no shortcut through this time I'm afraid, but I promise, it will ease."

Bethany nodded. "I feel as though right now, I'm trapped in the indigo stripe of the rainbow. I love the colour indigo so the analogy itself feels weird!, but it's this strange region, so narrow that many people can't perceive it yet it seems like a vast hidden dimension within the other colours. Cyan should be in there with the recognised colours too; it's as visible to me, and including it would save indigo from being the odd one out, the only one that isn't in a neat structure of primary and secondary colours. Some modern interpretations of the rainbow colours include cyan, but it appears to be presented as a choice between that and indigo; there should be room for both, but indigo is being pushed out! Maybe that's why I relate to it. Anyway, what am I like with my random digressions? Yeah, I'm definitely in the indigo band now. A strange, liminal zone outside of the clear simplicity of the others. I have this thing where I've been thinking of it as a transition before the stability of violet; a time of peace, being settled, everything recognisable and what's ahead being a much more steady flow through towards ultraviolet. No more drastic upheavals. I mean, I know that life can and will hold big changes as long as we are alive. For now, it's a mental image I need; a thought screensaver, being in this bizarre but finite indigo band looking towards the long calm of the violet band. This passing time, this indigo time is violet eve. That's all. Fleeting like the eve of a birthday or any other night before a special day. It helps me, by associating it with happy thresholds like Christmas Eve, to assimilate the thought that there are good moments in this time too; happy moments, useful learning moments, unusual and unexpected moments of support and connection which you need to be in these sorts of times to come upon. Violet Eve. That's what this is."

Bethany blinked and looked around; the sensation of Emma holding her hand; the lights, sounds and smells of the pub interior all returned, nudging her into realising how hyperfocused she had become as she articulated what had grown within her as a largely wordless, visual concept. She searched the others' faces for an indication of whether she had made any sense. Tiredness and overwhelm had her ability to read the cues she sought firmly relegated to power saving mode.

"Violet Eve. I love that!"

"You should be on tour giving talks about that; you would help so many people!"

Her shoulders relaxed. The clarity of words was indeed what the occasion required.

"Blurple!"

Oh dear; perhaps she should leave that part off her tour manifesto. "That was what one of the people at the one stop shop said they used to call indigo when they were a child. It came back to me because it made us laugh so much. It's a fabulous blurt of a word and I guess that's what I did there! It was one of those days at the drop-in where the conversation flowed naturally and, although I'll never be a group-socialising person, it brought home to me how important it is to have access to that setting."

The intensity of the day dissipated on a wave of kind, safe hilarity into the fuzzy sheen of everyone else's everyday; chatter, clinking glasses, chiming phones, that 'blown in with the rain and infused into the warmth' smell clinging to everything.

Chaotic and surreal as this era in her life was, it would appear she was in the zone where she was supposed to be after all.

14

Belonging

"Hi, Bethany; I'm glad you could get through here before Lucy goes back to Caithness for the rest of the holidays"; Charlene Sutherland ushered her and Lucy inside. "I'm so sorry about your dad, Beth. How are you feeling?"

"I'm not too bad, thank you; extra tired, I think that's going to take a while to ease and in some ways I feel as though it hasn't properly hit me yet but right now I mostly feel an increased thankfulness for my friends and my work. I need that sense of purpose; something to keep honouring my dad. Oh, hey Cheminot!"; she bent to stroke the big ginger cat who ran to greet her, his paws pattering on the light green linoleum as he came out of the kitchen. As she straightened up again, a tall dark-haired man in black jeans and a burgundy shirt which matched the frames of his spectacles brought some empty cans through from the living room. Bethany recognised him from recent posts on Brandon and Charlene's social media pages.

"This is Ethan, our cousin."

He greeted Bethany with a smile, indicating towards the fridge and asking if she and Lucy would like a can from the pack of lagers he had brought to share with Brandon.

"That's really kind, Ethan; thank you, but I've brought a couple of bottles of wine."

"No problem! Lucy?"

"Actually I wouldn't mind a lager, please; it's refreshing in this muggy weather. We were speaking about it as we walked back here from the station."

"Yeah, thanks for coming out to meet me off the train, Lucy. There's something about being met at the station; I don't know, something enduringly feelgood."

"Ah, yes; there's still that buzz around the railway and people getting together", nodded Ethan.

"I gather you're a train enthusiast as well? You'll fit right in here!", said Bethany as she set her bag with the wine on the kitchen worktop. Ethan Sutherland had become close to Brandon and Charlene since she got in contact during her family history research. Brandon would always need support with any change to his routine, but with their parents having relocated abroad, the energy costs of the large family home were becoming prohibitive. As Ethan worked freelance from home in the field of graphic design, since the cousins had hit it off he was making regular visits in preparation for eventually moving in. Bethany waited for him to get out fresh cans for himself, Brandon and Lucy, then put the Pinot Grigio she had brought into the fridge. Charlene invited her to pour the two of them a glass each from a Chardonnay she already had chilling and they all went to sit in the comfort of the large living room.

The room held a mix of old-fashioned cabinets, bureau and sideboard with more neutral modern seating, coffee table and a folding dining table. The combination had come together over many years, but felt natural; open and welcoming, with the different shades of wood reminiscent of a forest filled with unhurried life.

"So, Beth, I wanted to give you this photo at the funeral but I thought it might be a bit too poignant and not the right place, and I didn't know whether you'd have anything suitable on you to put it in"; Lucy took out an envelope from the patchwork tote bag on the couch beside her, holding it out to Bethany. Inside was a photograph; evidently a recent copy of a much older image from early in the previous century, of a frail-looking woman holding a tiny baby.

"From the date on the original of this, Charlene is certain that this is Harriet, being held by her grandmother Vicky Sutherland who died very soon after she was born. She wanted you to have a copy of it, because I know…" conscious of tact and the recent occasion, Lucy's voice faltered for a moment; "…that Harriet was, is, important to you too."

"It's OK, Lucy; you can say it. She knows I saw Harriet's ghost when I was ten! Diane and I always talk about 'Harriet moments' when meaningful coincidences happen!"

Bethany gazed in wonder at the baby in the photograph; the youngest of eight siblings who lived out her all too brief life in Charlene and Brandon's half of the house in the early twentieth century. The pair were descended from her brother Alexander. Building work carried out in the attics five years ago when Aunt Carole moved out of the other half of what was originally one property had resulted in Harriet's diary being found; it had given insights into her life which made sense of an apparent paranormal connection to Bethany and later to Lucy.

The newborn Harriet Eleanor Sutherland gazed out from the fragile layers of the past through the gloss of the photo paper; a depth and knowing to her eyes which belied her infancy. An old soul; one who would feel as deeply as the unmapped ocean floor and as keenly as a cut from a new blade, carrying the weight of big emotions even in the ten years she would be granted of this life. One whose sense of justice and vastness of empathy would transcend her untimely death, leaving those whose lives she touched through the ages wondering what she could have accomplished had she reached adulthood and had a robust support network of her own.

"Lucy, Charlene; thank you so much. This means a lot. I can hardly believe I'm looking at her as she was when she was here; the way everyone around at the time would have seen her, as a real, solid person! So Ethan, are you descended from Alexander Sutherland too?"

"No, from his brother Ernest. He and James were the twins. They adored Harriet; she used to tag along with them on their fishing trips. Their sons; my grandfather and great-uncles all grew up like brothers too and I loved hearing their passed-down stories when I was a kid. Ah, little Harriet. Breaks my heart thinking of what happened and it nearly destroyed my great-grandfather and James. Sorry, Bethany, I shouldn't be talking about that so soon after your dad."

"No, it's fine; I always enjoy hearing about the family history. We're distantly related to the Sutherlands from Harriet's generation onwards as you probably know, Lucy and me, through their mother Elsie; my grandfather Isaac was the son of her cousin who moved into the other half of this house when it was divided. I'd love to hear more about Harriet."

"Ah yes, Charlene told me we're remote cousins! Well, Harriet could be so intense and serious, they used to joke that she should have been the one to be called 'Earnest'!, but she was lively and interested in things. She loved being shown the techniques of baiting and casting and so on; she would get frustrated when she couldn't get the hang of it, but then she was equally happy sitting for hours watching them; listening to the sounds of nature and their boys' talk. She'd join in quite out of the blue, sometimes with the most random things! One time, she'd suddenly come out with 'I dreamed last night that I was a man, and I was very sad', and she went on to describe this whole scenario where she was standing beside a big wide river on a dull day looking up through the mist at a massive crane. Somehow she knew that it was in Glasgow, and she was a young man working in the shipyards but she was about to lose her job because 'things were going to change at the big yard'. She'd never been to Glasgow; I don't know how she'd even have seen pictures, but according to the twins, what she described matched the Finnieston Crane; the first one from the 1840s, not the later Stobcross one that became known by that name."

Before Bethany or Lucy could draw breath to say how interesting this was, Brandon looked up from his tablet. "That was Uncle Dùghall!"

"Hey, right enough!", exclaimed Charlene, "That would make sense! He did get made redundant from the shipyards before he moved up to Aberdeenshire. He found a new career on the railways; he became the Station Master, as it was known in those days, at Strathruan Station near Banchory. Sorry, Lucy, Bethany; this is Vicky Sutherland's maternal uncle we're talking about. Dùghall Strachan. We call him uncle because, well, it's pretty cool for us having a relative who was a Station Master!"

"Yes, Diane said something about you finding out about him. Didn't he run the station with his sister?"

"He did. Vivien Strachan. He sent for both his sisters when he got himself established; their parents died fairly young. Neither he nor Vivien ever married; they seem to have been a happy team, content with their lives in a peaceful place. Their younger sister, Ruby, married Brodie Chatto and they were Vicky Sutherland's parents. Brodie's own sisters married and moved away; to Dundee and Nairn, I believe, so he enjoyed having Ruby's siblings settled close by. Vicky loved visiting her aunt and uncle at their station in the summer when she was a teenager"; Charlene smiled wistfully. "I always get the sense of a golden age when I think of them. I believe it's called anemoia; nostalgia for a time one has never known. I think it's a state with which a lot of people who love the railways in this day and age are familiar."

Bethany felt an ache of understanding as she and her friend exchanged looks before Charlene glanced over towards her brother, now absorbed in his tablet once again.

"I always feel that in Perth Station"; she allowed the quiet moment to pass before breaking the lull in conversation. "I'm so lucky to get to call that cathedral of a place my local station. It feels as though every square millimetre of it is packed with the buzz and brightness of journeys past. Walkways that hardly anybody uses any more, archways, old clocks, dormant doors that look as if they're hibernating, all dwarfed by that massive roof; traces of old patterns, old ways. It's all still there, locked in time, but every part of the place is breathing; the slow, barely heard breath of deep sleep, but ready to come alive at any moment into a new age where everything feels positive again. Crisp exciting mornings; bustling varied days; calmly settling evenings. There's a footbridge far along connecting Platforms 3 and 4, nowhere near the exit now and the main one has ramps so I hardly ever see it used; it feels to me like a crossing over point into that long-ago heyday. Perth needs a station cat. Ideally a seal point Siamese; it would match the brown and cream, and the grandiosity." She looked around, abruptly conscious of having well and truly gone off on one but saw universal interest and approval. "Imagine the racket it would make, mind you; a Siamese cat yowling away in all that echoing space! Plus it would probably get stolen."

The doorbell chimed as they all laughed.

"Ah; that will probably be Diane"; Charlene got up to answer the door. Brandon and Ethan got up to go for a walk on the promenade, intending to get some chips from Vinny's seafront shop on their return; breaking up the bouts of group social energy was an important part of Brandon's coping, however accepting and cordial the company. Diane smiled a greeting as they passed her.

"Hey, Di; how was your workshop in Edinburgh?"

"Pretty good; I enjoyed hearing about people's creative ways of coming up with what reasonable adjustments would work for them. Being a part of something can help some people, if it's managed properly, and although many of us would never be able to sustain mainstream employment, a good work coach can make a difference to those who can or feel they could try, as long as the work coaches are properly informed and supported too. It can't be an easy job, all the understandable fear directed at them; it was a good reminder that they are people with feelings and vulnerabilities too. Sally enjoyed the event as well; I'm lucky to have her as a supervisor. She's a reassuring presence for moral support with my anxieties around timing, interrupting without realising, not catching what someone says, all the pitfalls that go along with big group events. She never makes me feel small, or like her good deed for the day, or a prop to show how inclusive she is. She never talks over me or for me; never rolls her eyes or does that 'oh, *you*' hand flap thing if I have a glitch. She takes me seriously. I'm not Diane the token neurodivergent rep; I'm Diane the colleague, who happens to be autistic and therefore I know what I'm talking about. She's excited for us about how interested Magnus is in the autistic hygge idea; I've to keep her posted. And the journey back! We got to Waverley Station and the LNER Aberdeen train was pulling in. That one doesn't stop in Inverbrudock, but it was the 'You Belong' Azuma; the one they put vinyls on one end to advertise their partnership with Campaign Against Living Miserably. I've seen the 'Celebrating Scotland' one there a couple of times, but never this one. So I was jumping up and down squealing about this to Sally, saying how important it is to me to have that message about mental health and belonging going about on the network and I wanted to get a photo of it there for you and Brandon too. I knew he'd be ready for a break by the time I got here so that's why I didn't say anything at the door; I'll show him when they get back, or message them to you. Anyway, I got a couple of photos and Sally said, 'have you travelled on it?' And I said I hadn't yet but it was on my goals list, so she said, 'well, we've got open tickets; you can just change at Arbroath to the train we would have been on anyway!' So we did, and I got a couple more photos at Arbroath! How cool is that?"

"Di, that's brilliant! I know how much you wanted to get a journey on that train", said Bethany as both she and Lucy gave fist pumps of sheer joy.

"Thank you for considering Brandon's social energy levels too", put in Charlene as she handed Diane a glass of wine. "We were talking about railways as it happens; Ethan had told us about a fascinating dream Harriet once described to Ernest and James, which they had always remembered and the story was passed down"; she filled Diane in on the incredible details.

"Well, isn't that so interesting? And she picked up that Dùghall, as it does sound likely it was him, was sad because of losing his job? That's astonishing for such a young child. It had to be a memory she was getting, surely."

"Actually, I emailed an update to Marion when we found out more about that generation", Charlene referred to another cousin with whom her research had brought her into contact, "and I'm not sure that would have been the only reason Dùghall was sad. Although he genuinely seemed to have been happy with his bachelor life and the company and best friendship he had with Vivien, apparently there had been a girl in Glasgow; Eloise. Whether they had a romance or were friends or acquaintances is unclear, but she married someone else. Marion gathered from what she heard that it wasn't a question of him pining away; he simply never met anyone who could replace her and he didn't need to force it because he was happy with his new life. The railway; the area. He most likely took the chance primarily for the sake of a potential better life for his sisters when some contact or other gave him the opportunity to go for a different job in a new place, rather than to escape the scene of a broken heart. It certainly worked out for him, but there's no doubt it would have been a huge emotional upheaval for him to leave."

Diane raised her glass in a knowing salute.

"Well, I have to say, however many decades ago this was, I'm delighted that it worked out for him and nobody, that we know of anyway, tried to pressure him to force a second choice relationship. Presumably because he didn't display any signs of being dysfunctional as a result of his heartbreak; he was fortunate enough to find a stable situation which was genuinely compatible with his needs and his physical and mental fitness."

Bethany nodded vigorously.

"You are so right there. Today, he'd be expected to prove he had gotten over Eloise. You know, many of a whole generation of women lost 'the one' to war, and it was accepted if they never replaced him. Why shouldn't it be as valid an option for a man? I'll admit, too, that hearing this as recently as a few months ago I'd have been tempted to wonder if he was on the asexual spectrum. Maybe he was. But does it matter? He didn't owe anyone an explanation. It needs to be enough that he was happy; from what you've said, Charlene, not one thing in his life after he left Glasgow could have been described as a reluctant compromise or avoidance or whatever baggage people would attach to it nowadays. I've been thinking a lot about labels recently; about them being tools, not prisons, and about them being protected by our right to boundaries; for us to use at our own discretion with honesty, not something we somehow need to earn by manipulating our own inner truth. About gatekeeping and how harmful it is. And I think pressure to justify anything and everything which doesn't match up to normative expectations, even within the LGBTQIAP+ community, is a big part of that. Labels get distorted because people are put in the position of needing to declare them in order to protect themselves from coercion, then they get attacked from within the community of that label for not being it enough; accused of diluting its meaning. 'Pick a side'; 'you're just confused and don't know your own mind'; 'you need to try harder'; 'you just haven't done enough Personal Growth, you don't know what's good for you'. One of the hardest things for many people to get their heads around is that for someone who has had experience of lost love, like Dùghall with Eloise, healing and ideal outcomes *can* entail a path which does not lead to another sexual and / or romantic relationship. Just because someone is, or has been, capable of falling for someone in that way, it doesn't mean that the only possible way they can recover from loss or rejection and have a good life is to fill that gap with something in kind. We all know, or at least we jolly well should know, the absolute supremacy of consent; that no means no. It just tends to get conveniently forgotten when someone's healing doesn't follow that expected path towards a replacement."

Diane's eyes had been focused intently on Bethany throughout her words.

"Yes, I agree. I think you're talking about when someone has reached out for support, or been referred, because of a pattern of unsuccessful attachments and the assumption is that those happened because of some blockage preventing them from 'building a healthy, reciprocal relationship'?"; the air quotes were clear in Diane's intonation and wry facial expressions. "And that society favours the rigid belief that the only way forward, the sole acceptable outcome, is a lukewarm relationship with resigned acceptance of no excitement, the feelings not happening naturally and having to force it despite a lack of attraction, since the person's judgement has failed to pass muster so they have forfeit the right to say no if not attracted? And that the professionals, therapists, driving this corrective path are missing the fact that some people have had destructive attachments as a result of the conditioning we all receive, that the right way to be happy and fulfilled and complete and to overcome any sense of life not working out is through succeeding at sexual and romantic relationships. When in actual fact that is not right for them at all, hence being drawn to unattainable targets. When there may be another reason such as neurodivergence or a medical issue making their life not work out but that source of unmet need lies undetected underneath the default explanation that they're not 'getting it right' with the obligatory love life, or they have 'unrealistic expectations'. And *if* that lack of ability to fall for a 'suitable' prospect is eventually linked to unrealised asexuality and aromanticism, those attachments which brought them to need support rule them out of inclusion by other aspec people because of gatekeeping?"

"Yes; that's correct, and raises an important point in that it's not only people who feel no or limited attraction who have the right to choose their path. Allosexuals and alloromantics are every bit as entitled to seek a future which doesn't involve a relationship; to set a boundary in that what they lost cannot be replaced, and to have that boundary respected. Other people may disagree; they are entitled to hold the *opinion* that there could be another love in time, but nobody has the right to try to *enforce* that. I'm saying that I'm glad for Dùghall's sake that he lived in a time when he had the options and the psychological privacy to find his own way, in his own time, to his own solution which was not what gets forced on people who have lost in love today. Though of course, the other side of that coin is that there was less belonging for LGBTQIAP+ identities in that era."

"I'm glad for Dùghall too, that he had such a lovely life", interjected Lucy; "and listening to both of you, I am profoundly thankful that I live in a time when there is so much more understanding that nothing is that simple when it comes to labels, thanks to the openness, emotional hard work and risk taking other people like you have put in. I know we can't have everything, but I'd love to see it come full circle; to reach a stage where those of us who identify with a specific label can do so, where labels can be inclusive and flexible where needed without it making people afraid of their own identity being diluted or erased - and if they are, that concern is valid and needs to be accommodated. But also, to be in a world where nobody needs to declare a label in order to have their boundaries honoured. It sounds complicated but simply amounts to 'live and let live'!"

"Well said, Lucy. If being excluded from an identity by overzealous gatekeeping makes you feel hurt rather than relieved, chances are you do belong", asserted Diane; "and like Bethany says, labels work for us, not us for them."

"Quite right", Charlene said firmly, "and I expect Dùghall would have agreed with all of that. Even if he could in theory have gone on to have another relationship which would have put Eloise out of his mind, what's the harm to him or anyone else that he didn't? Every life has a multitude of paths not taken, and some of them would have worked out better than what was chosen. As you've all acknowledged, he was happy. It's nobody else's business. Looking at what we know of his life and what I know of your experiences brings it home how fortunate he was to be allowed to find his own way. Vivien too; she was just as content and lived a good life. There's no evidence to suggest that either of them held the other back"; a hint of emotion gently rocked Charlene's words. "They went with the flow, and I love it. They had their country station, their rowan trees from which Strathruan got its name, their cottage which was practically at the end of the platform, and yes, there was a station cat."

A chorus of "Really?!"s erupted as a smiling Charlene made them wait while she went to the fridge; after she replenished three wine glasses and brought Lucy the can of Irn Bru she asked for, she resumed her ancestors' story.

"He was a character by all accounts. Pure black with odd-coloured eyes; one blue, one golden yellow. Heterochromia is fairly rare anyway and extremely uncommon in a black cat, but he had it. He came from a litter the family at the post office's cat had; Vivien went to post a parcel and came home with this kitten. They named him Obsidian; Sid for short. He would follow Dùghall up and down the platform when he was doing his duties, greeting passengers and jumping up into the carriages; he was taken away with the train a few times, but the crews all knew him and would make sure he got safely home. Strathruan was on the Deeside Line; Queen Victoria travelled through there a few times. There was a story that Sid got into the Royal carriage and made off with a fillet of salmon from the Queen's plate once!"

"No *way*!"

"Actually, Lucy, you're probably right; historical accounts of that time tell us that Queen Victoria never ate on board a train. She believed it was bad for the digestion. I suspect that was the nineteenth century rural Scottish equivalent of an urban myth; it wouldn't surprise me if Sid got into the Royal Hotel kitchen down the road and pinched a salmon from there, possibly one being prepared for a Royal visit and that escapade was embellished over the years. He lived to be at least fifteen; I say at least, because he eventually disappeared. We know, sad though it is for their people, that cats often go away when they sense it is their time. But when Marion was telling me all this, her understanding was that Vivien always said he had gone on somewhere else; that he was travelling onwards as a true railway spirit, turning up wherever he was meant to be."

Bethany swallowed a lump in her throat as she reached down to pet Cheminot, who was carrying on that railway family feline tradition by appearing right where and when he was needed.

Brandon and Ethan's reappearance in due course with the chips rounded off the evening. A few of those, fluffy and golden direct from the brown paper, warmed Bethany's insides and soaked up the moderate amount of wine she had drunk; enough to leave her with no more than a background glow for the journey home. Diane offered to walk her to the station.

"Could we stop off at the Fulmar's Nest?", asked Bethany. Diane nodded; her knowing, empathic smile told Bethany that this was expected after the intense conversation sparked by the revelations about Dùghall and Eloise. "I want to talk to you about something. I had a good chat with Des when he gave me a lift home before the funeral, and he helped me to sort out a few things I've been afraid to share about my past."

15

A Long Held Secret

"Thanks, Helen"; Bethany and Diane both smiled at the manager of the Fulmar's Nest, Inverbrudock's biggest seafront pub, as she brought over a fresh round of wine and the card machine.

"Give me a shout if you do want any more drinks", Helen grinned knowingly as Diane tapped her card to make the contactless payment.

"This will have to do us for tonight; I'm heading back to Perth and working tomorrow!"; Bethany grimaced slightly knowing that there would be a big fatigue debt to pay in the morning. She was below her limit but above her comfort zone where 'school nights' were concerned. Sometimes that lower limit could be tested; bereavement had sharpened her need not to end up looking back on a life where she had never stretched her energy capacity for the sake of the occasion. Especially the unplanned ones; the get-togethers which happened organically. Those were the best. She looked out at the ever present yet ever shifting blown-glass tableau of the North Sea, shown to full effect through the towering first floor windows; watched by an equally dynamic procession of customers as they met and took refreshment and shared.

"Beth, I'm honoured that you've trusted me with this; of course I'm not offended that you told Des first. I'm glad he was there and in a situation where you felt able to get the words out aloud, and I understand why you felt more able to disclose to someone with whom you have less intense shared history and confidences than you do with me. I'm just sad in that I could have been supporting you with this! You don't owe me an explanation, and you certainly don't need to measure up to me in terms of lack of one type of attraction or another in order to 'qualify' as aromantic as well as asexual! See, this is exactly why gatekeeping makes me so angry! Attraction is nuanced anyway. Some people enjoy the imagining but wouldn't want it to happen, including with the person or people to whom they're attracted. That would fit with being lithosexual if you wanted to seek a more precise label, but it is still part of the asexual spectrum, and likewise with feeling something you interpret as romantic within the aromantic spectrum. And if your feelings are experienced for a vanishingly small number of people, as in your case, even if you did want it to happen, that rarity of people to whom you're attracted counts too. In any case, whatever the nature of your experience of attraction and which label it may or may not fit closely under, it's not wrong and your boundaries hold sacred, always."

"I'm so relieved you don't feel I've deceived or betrayed you by not telling you; that I haven't appropriated your identity or faked an aspec space in our friendship by identifying to you as asexual and aromantic without qualifying it. I was more afraid of that than of the historical attractions having been wrong in themselves; I know that's not the case, and I get that orientation is about 'attraction not action' anyway."

"And it's none of my business unless you choose to share it with me! You have proved yourself a safe friend, as have Des and Jason who don't seek to identify any way because they're simply not bothered and are happy with their lifestyle as it is; as has Sharon who is in a relationship with a non-binary partner, Kate who is married to a man, Priya who is married to a woman, Cherilyn who is aromantic and allosexual, and so on. What I share with you, I would share regardless of your own orientation, because you are my friend and I trust you. Yes, I can expect you to empathise more with my own aroace identity because of your experience, but you've told the truth about that; about the basics of how you feel. You wouldn't be having these conversations if you were allosexual and alloromantic, Beth."

"I think I've been worried that I might have appropriated the aroace identity to try to protect myself from coercion. As happened to you when your hero-worshipping of Verena was misinterpreted; the kind of pressure we were all saying that we're glad Dùghall seems to have been spared by the happy life he was able to build for himself after Eloise. Nobody should have to rely on an orientation for their 'no' to mean no; consent is sacrosanct. It's wrong to dilute and undermine a minority group by using it as a shield if I don't truly belong in it, and that's what I've been afraid I might stand accused of doing, even once I knew that asexuality and aromanticism are a spectrum."

"That's a form of imposter syndrome a lot of neurodivergent people experience; not only in matters of our orientation. It comes from years of being told that other people have the right to dictate our own limits; how and when we need support or adjustments, and what kind. That we're either too low down the problems hierarchy and should shut up and count our blessings and get on with it, or that we're completely incompetent, too clueless about our own minds to have any say and are going to have 'help' and limitations forced upon us."

"That makes sense; I hadn't thought of it in terms of imposter syndrome, but you're right. It is another example of self-doubt from conditioning, and also from exposure to all the extreme views and anger on social media. I know a lot of the anger and frustration comes from trauma, and the points need to be made, but sometimes they hurt and exclude, isolate and further traumatise the wrong people."

"Definitely. I've become more selective in my use of social media and which topics I allow to dominate my feeds. I've had to. I don't want to encroach on your bravery in opening up to me about your own history, but I have been through something similar. Nobody knows about this; not even Des and Jason, but I did have an attachment to one of my teachers. It's taken me until recently to fully understand what it was and what it wasn't. It was enough to be picked up on and get me into a lot of trouble. My parents were called to the school for a Serious Discussion because I hung around to talk to him, was miserable when he was going on sabbatical for a term and I was caught taking a pen from his desk. It was a cheap generic one; not a personal or valuable item, but he used it to write merit slips and I associated it with earning his approval. I only intended to borrow it to get me through the term when he wasn't going to be there, and slip it back onto his desk when he was due back. It was, nevertheless, technically theft. As you can imagine, all hell broke loose. My parents were so angry and disgusted; the teacher, well, I wasn't allowed to go near him or his classroom ever again, I was transferred to another set for his subject but I was told how disappointed he was in me. That he'd thought I was better than that and I had let him down by turning out to be 'nothing but a silly little girl and a sly thief at that'. To this day I have no idea whether he said that or people made it up to try to put me off him, but I took it literally at the time."

"Oh, Di. How old were you?"

"Thirteen. I was already being bullied; you can imagine what it was like when that came out. The rumour mill added the kind of extra details you can no doubt imagine; not on his part of course, nobody in their right mind would have thought he would touch me. No, I was meant to have made all kinds of clumsy, cringemaking passes at him. Even my parents believed I'd done more than I had. My siblings being so much older were already living away by that time and were never told the details; only that I'd done something very bad and foolish and embarrassed the family and they were not to hug me or show me any undeserved affection when they visited."

"Are you fu…"; Bethany glanced around the pub, cutting short the expletive as she noticed a family with young children nearby. With a huge effort, she lowered her voice; "Are you *kidding* me? Tell me they didn't comply?"

"Well, Adrian was never that affectionate with me anyway; he was incrementally more aloof than usual but that was about as much contrast as if someone spilt a bottle of Tipp-Ex down a ski slope. Georgina smiled at me a couple of times when our parents weren't looking; it wasn't much but it was a lifeline, though at the time I felt guilty for receiving it."

"Your sister smiled at you a couple of times and that was more kindness than a heartbroken thirteen-year-old deserved. Jeez, Diane."

"I will never forget the day I was marched home from school and sent up to my room. I knew then, more profoundly than any child should, that I was alone in this world; that I was a monster and a misfit. I had to be, for something I felt as love to turn out to be so evil and for me to deserve such hatred. My memory of the surrounding details is hazy but as I collapsed on my bed I could swear my life flashed before my eyes. You know, like it's supposed to right before you die? I saw, not my whole life, but a kind of patchwork of the weeks of the summer holidays unrolling like tickertape. I think, looking back, I knew I would never be free in the same way to be my natural authentic self again. In the weeks and months after that, what I now know to be my sensory sensitivity and autistic inertia both went through the roof. Everything was heightened; light throbbed; sound shrieked. I was constantly exhausted; I craved stillness like a drug. I curled up in my room and devoured articles and documentaries about far-off, remote places and tried to will myself there. In the Faroe Islands they have something called the 'Diamond Sound'; there's a guided walk to an isolated valley where you can hear it the same as it was when Irish monks first went there one and a half millennia ago. It's a combination of dripping water, wind and the cry of ravens. The undisturbed, unpopulated simplicity of it; the idea of a place so far from the interpersonal chaos of school and my family, called to the deepest reaches of my soul. I dreamed about it and woke up devastated that I wasn't there. It felt as though, if I could astral-project myself there, I would be free; none of this would have happened, my mind would be wiped like a blank cassette and I wouldn't be bad any more."

"Good grief. How dare people with a duty of care make a child feel like that? I can relate to the heightened sensory issues and fatigue; that Diamond Sound walking tour would have appealed to me too, but I wish I could go back in time and tell that little girl that she had done nothing wrong; to help her to understand the psychology behind her feelings."

"Oddly, it wasn't until the situation with Verena that I began to understand that all my attractions were alterous, although I'd had other more intense hero-worship attachments before her. A lot of that piecing together came out of my conversations with you at that time, which put me on the right path towards naming it. Because of the default heterosexual setting which I needed to unlearn, I had already asked questions of myself about what I felt for Verena that I wouldn't necessarily have asked had she been a man. There was an added element there of wanting female friendship, since at that time I only had Des and Jason as close friends. Plus of course the lifelong need for approval from older mentor figures. I never wanted to have sex with my teacher. Or snog him, grope him, walk around holding hands, and as for romantic dinners? Dear God, *eat* in front of him? I would have been more comfortable, and less likely to end up spectacularly choking, using a boa constrictor as a bungee rope! Everyone around me at the time described it as 'a crush' and assumed the conventionally understood meaning of that, so I internalised it and accepted that I must be in love with him. I had nothing to compare it to in my own experience and nobody to talk to who would have given me the knowledge to figure it out. I tried imagining the things people were saying I'd tried to get from him but I couldn't make those thoughts flow; I put that down to not having the experience to know what to imagine, and that fit with all the 'little girl knows nothing about life' putdowns I got all the time through talking and acting older than my years as so many unknowingly autistic girls do. I had seen enough on TV to be able to imagine kissing and cuddling, and I told myself that must be what I wanted; I didn't know to question it. I kept it so secret up to now not only because of the shame at the time and the stealing part, but because it felt desperately wrong as a piece of my history; to be obliged to believe that I had sexual feelings. I don't mean sinful; I mean not right for me. When I look back now truly knowing that I didn't, I can see that all I wanted to imagine was the warmth of reciprocal admiration and the rush of approval from on high. That what broke my heart was not being denied the prospect of any physical contact with him; it was the cutting off of emotional closeness as I perceived it. The loss of his endorsement of me and replacing it with something so dramatically opposite; contempt and anger. As an adult, I have an understanding of what happened; I wasn't 'a thief', I was a child with a lot of displaced intensity which led to misguided attempts to self-soothe, and the pen was a transitional object; a source of comfort and a stand-in for lost stability when my teacher was not going to be there for an entire term. And why I attached myself to him given that it wasn't sexual or romantic? Again it comes back to my being an undiagnosed autistic girl. Thinking, acting and talking older than I was, and as a kid that was inevitably a joke to all the adults around me. An affectation; an 'old head on young shoulders'; 'oh, just wait until you've lived a little'; 'lighten up' and so on. As a late addition to an established family with much older siblings and cousins, I was used to a setting where in my head I was a contemporary but I was never accepted as such because of my chronological age. At school, for all the bullying that went on, I was the same age as my peers and stood out in a different way by doing well academically and coming across as more mature in that sense; it made me a target, but my autistic social struggles were masked by already being an enemy because of being 'a swot' so that wasn't picked up. My academic work and the bullying connected to it doubly marked me out for a genuinely well-intentioned teacher to make an effort to encourage and support me. Which of course unwittingly tapped into a vacuum of intensity, dependence and devotion. He never did anything which could be called grooming; he was a good and moral educator. He would have been trained to look out for the signs of what is generally understood as 'a crush', but that was not me. He was probably horrified believing that he'd missed something which was a safeguarding issue. Which he had; they all had. Just not the issue they automatically assumed it to be."

"Hell's bells, Diane. I honestly don't know how you came through that time; being demonised like that for something so natural and understandable, so young and in complete isolation."

"Probably much the same way you did, Beth!"

"Fair point; we weren't given any choice, were we? Your thoughts were purer than mine, though…"

"No! I won't endorse you doing that to yourself. We so often fall, or get pushed, into this comparing trap. It's not a competition and that's another reason why so many of us miss out on support, healing and closure. Being guilted and shamed because we're made to feel that somebody else's story trumps ours or has less fault on their part. It also doesn't matter how carnal your thoughts were. I'm not having a go, Beth, truly; I understand. I'm trying to ease the pressure on you. You're dealing with the passing of your dad and it's exacerbated an earlier loss that was never healed; your ability to be authentic inside your own mind and sit with your feelings to get to know them without fear or shame was taken from you. I know the gist of that mental strain because of my own past; each of the children we were needs and deserves to be vindicated and to have that blame lifted. The supremacy awarded to sex over everything else in our society has created a sliding scale of outrage around attraction as experienced by anyone 'vulnerable', whether by age or disability, with sexual right at the top, yet it's no more or less natural than an absolutely platonic hero-worship. The emphasis ought to be on the damage, if any, being sustained to the person dealing with having intense unreciprocated feelings, not the nature of their private thoughts, or the perceived insult to their idol for that matter. Should their experience of attraction or attachment become negative or lead them into destructive or dangerous responses, they need compassionate guidance and help without trampling over their right to privacy, especially of their inner thoughts. Not punishment for 'having ideas above their station' and a lifetime of lingering shame, irrespective of how high up on the outrage meter their imaginings registered! What I'm getting at is, please don't add to the mental labour of all you're processing by telling yourself that I deserve healing more than you do because my alterous attractions and thoughts were 'cleaner' and less 'wrong'. I admit, I prioritised it not being sexual when I was challenged about Verena; some people around me jumped to conclusions that my attachment was sexually motivated and treated that as the main problem, so I had to construct my defence accordingly. It got in the way of my dealing with the real issue, which was the negative impact on my emotional wellbeing and working relationships. I needed to work out the alterous nature of it in order to know what I was dealing with and to recognise that the way in which I was being coerced to replace it was inappropriate for me, not because a romantic or sexual attraction should have been seen as any more problematic. It's high time we, as in society, looked at attraction differently."

"Well, I am glad that Verena's squeamish snobbery had some benefit for you in the end. I can't believe you've kept that secret about your teacher all these years; it makes so much sense when you talk about how your attachment to him came to be."

"Yeah, I might have to thank her one day; it would be worth it to see the look on her face! Making peace with the mechanism of my attachments is a work in progress; I'm still that child who was such a criminal for responding to an adult in my life finally taking me seriously and 'getting' me. My point in telling this story now is that we all need to look past the extremes and stereotyping within our own marginalised identities so that adults like us can recognise and make peace with their own back stories, and kids like us can be spared going through the same shit on their own that we did. You've done nothing wrong by not having felt able to share with your friends; you're as entitled to privacy as anyone else and no coming out is ever owed, but we're both a product of a society which has a hell of a lot left to learn about expectations and rigid, narrow categorising."

"If people could talk about their experiences without fear of judgement or gatekeeping, there would be so many more people who don't fit society's allonormative and amatonormative expectations finding belonging without anyone having to compromise their privacy and boundaries."

"Remind me; what's the difference between those two?"

"Allonormativity is the belief that people should experience so-called typical levels of attraction, be it pan, bi, homo or hetero; amatonormativity is the belief that everyone should want and seek the conventional idea of a love relationship. How do you feel now that you've told me your own experience?"

"A bit self-indulgent to be honest; you've just disclosed to me after having had a massive bereavement, many would say it was not the time to tell my own story."

"But Diane, it was so natural and right; it was beautiful and affirming for me. And bereaved people are allowed to share solidarity; everything we've talked about is a form of bereavement. Having barriers to knowing or being able to own your identity and your personal truth can lead to feelings of bereavement once you begin to put it all together, for the more authentic life you could have known. I think that's mostly why I ended up confiding in Des; the weight of the loss of my dad made it impossible to keep on carrying the other type of bereavement in secret. I dislike the word 'crush' because it has come to imply triviality, but it's apt in terms of the weight of the burden it can be. The attachments which went badly for us, and the massive chunk of ourselves we lost as a result, then that being compounded by gatekeeping and scepticism."

"Yes; you're quite right. Thank you. And how do you feel now?"

"Like a weight has been lifted and…"; Bethany quickly unlocked her phone and checked an app; "…my train's just ten minutes away from Montrose!"

"Ooh; that will be time to finish up then!"; they both drained their glasses and gathered their belongings, returning the empties to a grateful Helen at the bar before rushing out into the invigorating lift of night air at the end of a clouded summer day's oppressive heaviness.

16

Murray Dunsmuir

Stirling sparkled in the high heat of a wall-to-wall sunshine day. Sweat glazed the faces and bodies of tourists as they hauled suitcases up the steepening streets past the Golden Lion Hotel and up towards the Old Town, where the road divided into two at the end of King Street and the stately parade of historic streetlamps began. Bethany smiled as she thought of Diane and her aesthetic fascination with them; especially that kind, with the question mark shape and the hanging lamp which would illuminate at dusk in a glow of LED moonlight.

Mr Dunsmuir was expecting her in half an hour; she killed some time by walking up Spittal Street as far as the top of Baker Street Gardens, where she leaned on one of the lamp posts for a few moments to catch her breath after the uphill climb in sticky afternoon heat. The pale green top of the observatory attached to the Stirling Highland Hotel glinted across the street; a reminder of cool night air which gained substance in the solid metal of the lamp post as she looked up at the tapered glass lantern, imagining it lit in the temperate respite of evening. Hoping that nobody in the impressive white-harled, crow stepped gabled apartment building just beyond the lamp post was watching, she pulled herself away and went to sit for a few minutes in the shade of the tree-lined gardens. She distracted herself from the heat and her shortness of breath by imagining what it must be like to stay in that building; to have the view of the gardens and way out over the whole of Stirling, perhaps to sleep in a room which included the curve of the old stair towers that had jutted proudly out onto the street for hundreds of years. She checked her appearance in the compact mirror she kept in her handbag, hoping that she would not be embarrassingly red in the face when she arrived for her informal but businesslike meeting. Difficulty regulating her internal temperature may be a natural companion to her sensory sensitivity, but it did not pair so well with the unpredictable Scottish climate.

Bethany shrugged belatedly out of her light grey formal jacket, draping it over her arm taking care to avoid getting any marks on it or her pale peach maxi dress from the seat or the nearby foliage. She checked her phone for any messages and to ensure for the second time since getting off the train that she had remembered to switch it to silent mode. Satisfied, she put it away and took a few more moments to enjoy the lethargic breeze, the torpid moving shadows of the trees on the path and the sound of birds singing, before making her way back down the gentler gradient of Baker Street to where the two roads merged.

Dunsmuir and Ridley Solicitors had their office on the second floor of an imposing building just off Corn Exchange Road. A neutrally welcoming receptionist answered the entryphone and buzzed her in; she walked up a narrow staircase whose faded maroon carpet must have seen decades of apprehensive, hopeful and dejected footsteps, arriving at a light wooden door with a chunky metal handle which clicked open as the receptionist, who was friendlier in person than she had sounded on the muffled intercom and introduced herself as Leonie, heard her approach. She accepted the offer of a drink, turning down tea in favour of a glass of water; it arrived with the bonus of a couple of ice cubes and a welcome invitation that she could also feel free to have a cup of tea brought in when she was with Mr Dunsmuir. He would be free in about ten minutes, Leonie said; with apologies for the slight delay. Bethany always found it paradoxically reassuring when a professional was running late due to overrunning appointments; it suggested a thorough and client-centred style. She relaxed into a comfortable wooden-framed easy chair, her eyes following the subtle pattern of leaves in the rust-coloured carpet which looked much newer than that on the staircase.

"Bethany Sawyer?"

Murray Dunsmuir beamed an avuncular smile as he emerged through a door which was identical to the one by which Bethany had entered. He was a well built man, softened by late middle age but carrying it with style. He wore a light slate-coloured suit with a pale blue shirt and a silver tie with Royal blue stripes, knotted neatly but loosely as befitted the hot weather. A full head of silver hair offset rounded features; thick eyebrows the only facial hair he sported. He ushered Bethany through to his office, thanking Leonie for her offer of tea.

"So, my nibling, Blair, tells me that you have suffered a sad loss recently. I am so sorry; ah, what would you prefer me to call you?"

"Bethany is fine, Mr Dunsmuir, and thank you. Yes, my father died a few weeks ago; it was sudden, and as my mother had a cancer scare recently too, it has given me a lot to think about."

"Of course. Goodness me, how difficult for you. And you may call me Murray if you wish, though I appreciate that some people prefer to be more formal. Whatever feels right to you."

Bethany liked this man. A tight clench in the pit of her stomach which rarely felt able to let down its guard outside of her own home and the company of those in her closest circle began to relax a little.

"Thank you, Murray; I get that about formality, but I do feel safer when I'm allowed to be on an equal footing with someone who is helping me. I appreciate you making time for me; I must confess I'm feeling rather overwhelmed by all this"; to her horror, tears gathered to attention from nowhere and prickled into pole position behind her eyes. Murray nodded sagely, moving a box of tissues towards her and looking down to brush a non-existent fleck of dust from his tie in order to give her a moment of privacy.

"See, there is only me, and I am autistic. That makes the responsibility feel huge and my ability to perform as people expect me to feel infinitesimally small. I know it must seem a bit ghoulish of me to be thinking about my mother's mortality when I ought to be purely thankful that she's still here and currently well, but I need to be better prepared so that when that time comes and I have to do everything on my own, and when I will not have any spare capacity for taking in new information and instructions, I can have a better chance of doing her justice and performing well enough to make the rest of the family proud."

"Now, first of all, there is nothing ghoulish about preparing yourself for what will, one day, need to be done; for a fraught time in which you will have no choice as to when it arrives. You have done a brave and honourable thing arranging to come here today so soon after burying your father. I hear you about feeling the need to achieve a certain level of knowledge and, as you put it, performing, but both Blair and Emma have already painted a picture for me which I have no doubt is quite different from the harsh pen portrait you would draw of yourself. The other important thing you need to take away from our meeting today is that when that time does come, you will not be doing it all on your own. I and the various professionals with whom you will be interacting will be there to guide you; anyone working with bereavement has a duty of care to always remember how new and bewildering it can be, and how depleted people are at the point of having to deal with it. I'm not saying that everyone will get it right, but in terms of the administration tasks, what feels insurmountable to you is all in a day's work to them."

Bethany smiled tightly, her emotions on a firm leash as she absorbed the shift in the weight which had been pressing down on her; only now beginning to appreciate its magnitude as Murray continued.

"Now, you and your mother; that's Sheila Sawyer?"; she nodded in the affirmative; "have already been through the procedures of registering, informing and arranging the funeral of your father; Gerard? Gerard?"

"Gerald, but he went by Gerry."

"Ah yes; I heard of him as Emma's Uncle Gerry. So you already have some familiarity with the process, and although it must feel like a blur at this time, you will have taken in more of that knowledge than you realise. It will come back to you when you need it, though of course it makes a difference when you don't have another member of the immediate family; your household or that of the deceased, to help you. We can never rule out processes changing in the interim either; a small difference from what you remember of how things were done can feel enormous. Something which was dealt with by email last time may have to be a telephone call, or a document need to go to a different sequence of recipients. But we can all be thankful for how much is done online these days; it can be impersonal and it has its drawbacks, but it does mean that a lot more can be done from home. Scanned documents are becoming the norm too; you will have less requirement to present them in person. You will on occasion have to provide an original though, especially of the death certificate or the will; sometimes quite long afterwards. I do always recommend that people order, if they can afford it, several copies of the death certificate. All of those copies qualify as originals and you can send or hand one in without having to wait to get it back if you are asked for one by someone else."

"Yes, we did that with Dad's; it was recommended when we phoned to order it."

"Ah, good. That is definitely sound advice. And did the registrar point you in the direction of 'Tell Us Once' for informing all Government departments; tax, motor vehicle, pensions and so on?"

"Yes, zie did. Luckily my dad kept everything official so it was no problem finding his National Insurance number; we had come across it anyway when we were looking for his birth and marriage certificates and NHS card as well as the most recent letter from the Pensions Service to take with us."

"That's excellent. And you would have been told that it is now standard practice for the doctor or hospital to email their confirmation of cause of death directly to the registrar to speed the issue of the death certificate; if it is a sudden, unexpected or suspicious death, that does unavoidably add to the family's distress and the timescale but if there is any need for coroner or Procurator Fiscal involvement, they will keep all parties informed."

"Yes; that was all explained to us."

"Good. Now, the main thing which will be different when it comes to the time you need to face this regarding your mother is that you will need to know about confirmation. That means being responsible for the administration of the estate; what they call probate in England and Wales. Do your parents have a professional executor appointed?"

"Yes; they used a will writing specialist firm who are named as the executors."

"That is good news. But if you had ended up being executor, there would have been lots of specialised guidance and support available to you; I can email you some links to basic step by step guides about what happens when someone dies. It tells you about everything that needs to be considered; tax, debts, informing the bank and utilities, things like 'Tell Us Once' which we have already discussed."

"Yes please; that would be so helpful. I think the main thing I'm worried about it knowing what order to do things in as well as the details of each thing that needs to be done."

"Well, these guides take you through that step by step."

"Thank Goodness for that. And tax; what do I need to look out for around that?"

"Well, the main one is inheritance tax. Will there be a property to sell?"

"Yes; my parents own their house and I will not be wanting to move back into it."

"Right, and as far as you know, will there be a significant amount of other assets; money in the bank, life insurance, stocks and shares, other investments?"

"Nothing complicated; they had one joint bank account, no stocks and shares or anything like that. I don't know exactly how much is in the account; I don't feel it's my business to know that while my mother is still here, and anyway it won't necessarily be the same when her time comes. I hope that doesn't sound defensive; I do appreciate your help and I understand why you have to ask."

"Not at all, and I completely empathise; of course you want to respect your mother's privacy and autonomy. If the estate is liable for inheritance tax, the executor will need to deal with that first; there is a lower threshold and then a sliding scale. You would only ever pay tax on what is above that base amount which everyone has as a tax free allowance. The other types of tax you need to know about are income tax and capital gains tax. Again, your executor will talk you through that and they will be the ones to do the paperwork and pay it out of the estate, though they might need to ask you for information from time to time. You will need to check your own personal tax situation separately once you have inherited."

"I dread to imagine how people cope if there isn't an executor appointed and they have to do all this for themselves!"

"Even in that case, Bethany, there is always guidance available. The Citizens Advice Bureau would be a place to start. HMRC and all official departments have helplines; the banks and utilities have bereavement teams. Any outstanding debts, bills for utilities kept on in a property until it is sold; all of that is paid from the estate and the companies are accustomed to having to wait until the estate's assets are ready to be distributed. Funeral costs can be paid straight from the deceased's bank account too if it has sufficient funds; there are specific things for which banks are authorised to release funds and your funeral director can advise and liaise with the bank. There are bereavement benefits available for families facing funeral poverty in the event of the estate not having enough assets. If on the other hand the estate is valuable enough to be taxed, as may be the case with your parents, there will be enough to fund professional help for you to deal with it; fees for professional executors are payable from the estate after it is all settled and usually get deducted as part of their action."

"Well, that is a relief; I feel less afraid of being up against it on my own. What would these professionals need from me?"

"They would need a list of all assets and their estimated value; I believe it is only the total value of the estate which is required in England and Wales, but here in Scotland we do need those individual details. If anything is missed or discovered later, don't worry; there's a form for that too! It is understood that the next of kin does not necessarily know everything about the deceased person's financial affairs. As you rightly said about your mother, it is none of their business! And the processes, cold and daunting though they may seem, do take that into account. The important thing is to have a good line of communication with the professionals handling the administration, or with whoever is helping the bereaved to sort it out."

"That is so reassuring, and I'd be grateful if you could send me those links, please. A written step by step guide is what people need at a time like this; that and someone to talk us through it and also listen and accommodate the bereaved person's pace of thinking and understanding and processing. I can see that you have that down to a fine art; when the time comes, I would love to be able to check in with you?"

"But of course! Please do, and I will help you in any way I can. Don't worry if you struggle to remember all of this information; the links I'm going to send you will either directly cover it all or bring it back to mind. You need never feel ashamed of asking for help. As Blair always says, you are enough but you don't have to carry it alone."

"Seriously, thank you so much, Murray. I don't know Blair too well with them living so far away but they make my lovely cousin Emma very happy and I am so glad that they have you as their uncle."

"That's very kind of you to say. I hope they know that we're both proud of them. Howard, my older brother; Blair's father, often tells me how proud he is and when I ask him if he's said as much to them, he tends to demonstrate why Blair calls him 'a poster boy for stoicism'. If you know what I mean?"

"Indeed; I know exactly what you're saying. And don't worry; if Blair doesn't already know that their father is explicitly proud of them, they soon will. And by soon, I mean in about an hour's time when I message them an update from the pub before I get the train home."

Murray Dunsmuir nodded approvingly, his eyes holding admiration and acknowledgement as they met Bethany's before smoothly steering the conversation back to less intense topics.

"May I recommend the City Walls for your, ah…"

"One for the Railroad?"

"Indeed; a good way of putting it! It's on the Back Walk; the road leading down past the old walls, hence the name. Very popular with students, but at this time in the summer holidays it shouldn't be too busy. It's a magnificent example of architecture and is the kind of place where one can relax in grand surroundings; the best of both worlds."

"Now you come to mention it, I'm sure Diane - that's my best friend, she lives in Inverbrudock but grew up here in Stirling - has mentioned that place. We've recently been to Number 2 Baker Street, with Emma and her oldest sister Sharon; after my dad's funeral. I loved it there, but the name 'City Walls' is definitely familiar too."

"Number 2 is a wonderful hostelry; a good real ale pub. You go wherever you feel comfortable; you've had a lot to take in."

"Sure, but I would like to try this City Walls place today. I will pop in there; thank you."

Bethany put away her notebook, placed her cup on Murray's desk and gathered her bag and jacket, thanking Leonie on the way out for a perfect cup of tea. She exited the building into the lingering, less aggressive heat of a sun-washed early evening.

She found the Back Walk easily; it meandered downhill off to the left from where a flight of steps to the main road was illuminated halfway down by a solitary streetlamp with a distinctive old-fashioned post sporting a crosspiece cut short at one side, giving it an almost rakish appearance. It was topped by a frosted glass bowl of the more modern type whose light usually shone a pale pinkish colour, almost close enough to touch from the steps. Bethany surmised that this was one she recalled Diane describing and telling her how it had thrilled her to discover on an autumn visit that it in fact shone the deep amber of sodium light. She took a quick photo to send to her, smiling to herself at how much aesthetic detail she found herself noticing about streetlights since they became friends; she had to agree that there was something magical about a streetlamp whose light was an unexpected colour. The entrance to the City Walls was set into the high mediaeval boundary on the left hand side as she walked down the road; an archway discreetly inset by a modern glass door with a traditional sandwich board outside. Expecting an already full cosy nook of an establishment, Bethany pushed open the glass door and walked in.

The clang she heard was either the empty bottles being tipped into the recycling box or her own jaw hitting the flagstones. A short flight of steps, a lift at the side, led up into a vast bustling venue with timeless brick arches dwarfed by a high ceiling; the sun flooded in from a cornflower blue sky through skylights and tall windows. This place was huge! How did it fit into a wall? Pool tables, big screens and a myriad of different sections where people could sit in peace or gather in groups fanned out in all directions; strips of LED lighting at floor level gave each area its own distinct mood, from cosily secluded green through to warm bustling red. She could have sworn she had seen a notice about a roof terrace next to a long flight of stairs on the right when she walked in. She made her way to the fairy lit sweep of bar which formed the heart of the pub and smiled at the young, dark-haired man who came to serve her. Ordering a well-earned dram, she complimented the place and the barman's face lit up as he enthused about its recent refurbishment, pointing out the randomly mixed shades of the new hexagonal floor tiles which ranged from cream through hues of biscuity brown to dark chocolate. He confirmed that she had not imagined it; there was indeed a roof terrace too. Thanking him, Bethany took her drink to a quiet corner table with a promise to both herself and the barman that she would take the next one up to the terrace in order to get the full experience of the place.

Settled at her table, she took out her phone and updated her people on how well the day had gone; her first message was to Emma. The sky-high expanse of the City Walls was just about enough to hold her emotions as she conveyed the precious words for Blair regarding their father; the clarity and perspective of bereavement sharpening her awareness of what a privilege it was to be placed to give Blair this feedback while both they and their father were still in this world. Her phone was already pinging with replies as she drained her glass; laughing to herself, she determinedly folded the case over it and put it away in order to take the glass back to the bar, order a second and take it up to the roof terrace.

The long, narrow staircase opened onto a square of tables surrounded by decorative greenery and strings of big light bulbs which made Bethany wish it were September; a continental feel to the scene, with dormant but ready outdoor heaters adding a pragmatic Scottish touch. Music played through mounted speakers; a vibrant link to the bustling scene below. She sat in the shade of the stone wall, pulling out her phone once more; Murray had already emailed her several helpful links to step by step guides, emphasising again how well she was doing and what a pleasure it had been to meet her. She sent off a brief and businesslike reply, thanking him again for his help and all of his recommendations; she smiled to herself as she hit Send, confident that he would recognise the scope of 'all your recommendations' as she discreetly raised her glass from this revelation of a rooftop terrace. Silently, she acknowledged her father's spirit and her renewed closeness to her mother; gave thanks to the serendipitous gift of a rare, uniformly settled lapiz lazuli sky on such a personally meaningful Scottish summer day.

17

Two Months Later

Violet Eve: Stirling

"Thank you for coming, Bethany; I know you're commuting this week and it will have been a string of long days for you"; Miriam folded her dark green gilet over the back of the chair.

Unorthodox Roasters, to which Bethany had been initially drawn as much by the name as by the smell of artisan coffee, was in a lull between busy spells and the waiter brought their Americanos promptly. Bethany smiled at the sight of their trademark mutedly colourful cups; her coffee was in a mustard yellow one, Miriam's in a dusky blue one. Her cousin's broad fingers looked slightly awkward hooked through the small geometric handle; Bethany's fit snugly as she breathed in the aroma, earthy with a hint of cinnamon and clove.

"It's OK; I've enjoyed the novelty of working in the Stirling branch for a week though I couldn't take on a commute like this permanently. They've been so grateful to me for agreeing to do it at short notice; they were stuck when three of them went off sick one after the other with this awful cold that's going around. Magnus knows better than to bombard me with 'are you sure's; he respects that I know my own mind and that my word has value. He trusts me when I say that I'm happy to give something a try, and knows I love a trip to Stirling. Olivia, the manager here, was so thankful too; she said that it was the least she could do to let me have an extra half hour before my lunch break when I said that you had been helping my mum so much and had asked to meet me."

"That's good; I'm glad I haven't caused you any trouble at work. I only have an hour's parking anyway"; Miriam sipped her coffee. "Oh, this is good. I must let Bo know about this place. The colour scheme is quite distinctive too, isn't it?"

"Yes, I love the contrast of the light from the table lamps and the dark blue wall"; Bethany indicated the swan necked reading style lamp which gleamed brightly on the unvarnished, natural grain of the table. "So, how are you, Mim; what is it you needed to talk about?"

"It's nothing for you to be concerned about regarding Sheila; don't get worked up", Miriam crisply told Bethany who had thought she was doing a good job of controlling her ruminating on why her salt of the earth but not personally close cousin needed to ask her for a meeting. Oh well. "It's just that we may not be able to remain as involved as we have been. Bo's mother is showing signs of dementia."

"Oh, Miriam. I am so sorry to hear that; it must be upsetting for you both as well as concerning. Of course I understand that you will need to focus on her. Does Mum know?"

"Not yet; don't mention it to her, please."

"Which is why I was asking if she knew."

"Of course. I'm sorry; that came out more sharply than I intended."

"Look, we both appreciate everything you've done, as would Dad, and I hope you will keep in touch; Mum always enjoys your visits, you don't have to be doing anything for her to see her socially. I know you and I see the world in significantly different ways; we're never going to move in the same circles, but I genuinely am concerned about your news and care about how both of you will be feeling."

"Thank you, Bethany. Sheila does seem to be doing well and the doctors are happy as you know to monitor her every six months; I know you have been conscientious about keeping in contact and making sure she has what she needs. And Bethany, I realise; Bo and me both, that we haven't been the easiest people for you to turn to when you have had to approach us"; Miriam cleared her throat, taking another long swig of her coffee. "The fact is, that dreadful head cold you mentioned that's struck down your colleagues here? Well, we both had it and it floored me in a way that everyday illnesses rarely do. It affected my hearing for a while. Although it's gone back to normal now, I had a few experiences of struggling on the phone, and in somewhat fraught circumstances too. It hit me that this may be similar to what you have described, though I know in your case it's auditory processing rather than hearing as such. I confess that I am rather ashamed of not having taken seriously what a challenge it is for you, and an ongoing one. I only had it for a week or so. When Bo and I talked about it, we realised that if we'd gotten our understanding of that wrong, we'd probably done you an injustice in other ways too. We read a few articles as you suggested, and we both realise that we need to do better at listening to what you have been telling us; that it shouldn't have taken me happening to experience something slightly similar for us to make an effort to understand more."

Bethany risked a quick glance out of the window; no flying pigs could be seen in the blue-grey autumn sky above Friars Street. Stirling went about its business; people passed by, collars turned over hunched shoulders as though autonomously sensing the seasonal shift borne in a settling lace of chilled droplets of rain too small to see.

"I appreciate you saying this, Miriam; I do hope you're both fully recovered now. And it means a lot that you made the time to read articles when things are taking a difficult turn on Bo's side of the family."

"Well, it's on us that we hadn't done it before now. We're rather set in our ways and too comfortable in our own circle of similar people, I admit."

"I guess in some ways I've done you an injustice too, by assuming that because you and Bo have life experience of being in a minority group and having had to fight for your rights to make a secure life and future for yourselves as a lesbian couple, you would empathise with me more easily in my own experience of not fitting in to society's norms. I should not have presumed that; it's treating you differently than I would have a heterosexual couple, and that is the definition of discrimination. My issues and circumstances are different from yours; I shouldn't have been additionally defensive around you all these years because of some misplaced sense of betrayal."

"Thank you for saying that; I guarantee you, and I don't expect I need to tell you, that there is plenty of prejudice within the LGBTQIAP+ community as well as among different minorities."

"Yes; there is lots of ableism within disabled communities too, and as you say, other prejudices thrive in our midst. I think what we both, all, need to take from this is to be more open to listening to one another going forward. And if I can help in any way, for instance with looking up resources about dementia; how music helps, ways of using the past to evoke memories, things like that, I'd be happy to."

"Thank you; that means a lot. And Sheila; she does have other people around her for if we become less available, I know. Just make sure you do keep up that close contact; she will always need your support more than she admits."

"Of course."

"So, is this your last day working down here? I expect you'll be glad of a rest at the weekend."

"Yeah; though I am getting the train straight to Inverbrudock after I finish at four today. My friend Diane, you may have seen her at Dad's funeral, invited me through to join her and her best mates Des and Jason for a Friday night curry at the guys' flat; she's been commuting this week too as she's been on a course in Dundee so we had this random idea that it would be fun to do a Friday night celebration like mainstream employed people do at the end of a traditional working week. Des is a sensational cook; they run a local café. I could have stayed over but none of us will want to make it a late one; Jason has a competition at his local gym the next day and Diane and I will obviously both be tired. I need to wake up in my own bed tomorrow and have the whole weekend quiet and routine."

"So Des and Jason, are they a couple?"

"No; they're brothers."

Miriam nodded; Bethany braced herself for either a barrage of romance-orientated questions about 'these male friends of Diane's' or a condescending lecture about travelling back on her own. Or both. She was willing to be open minded about this cousin, but expecting miracles remained off the table.

"Well, you and your friends enjoy your curry; you deserve it. Bo has a cousin who has been taking an interest in Asian cookery; we might be asking for some recipe hints from your Inverbrudock contacts!"

Well, what about that? She was happy to be proved wrong every once in a while. Especially in such a positive way.

An alarm beeped on Miriam's phone; at least she hoped that was the source of the noise which came from her cousin's pocket.

"That's my ten minute reminder for the parking meter. Now, you watch yourself getting home, young lady; there are some nasty people about."

Well, one miracle at a time then.

"You don't say!"; Bethany rolled her eyes and sighed. "So, Miriam, if you really want to, another thing to learn about autistic people is that the stereotype about uniformly trusting everyone and having no worldly awareness is…"

"Hey, I'd say that to any of my normal family members or friends!"

"Nonautistic. Not 'normal'. That is an important point of language."

"Of course; sorry, I should have known that was offensive. But what I said about you getting home is simply what I would say to anyone."

"That there are nasty people about, as if you didn't expect me to be aware of that basic fact of life at almost fifty years of age? Calling me 'young lady' too, when there's hardly a decade between us. This is precisely the sort of infantilising that grinds neurodivergent people down; each instance seems trivial in isolation but they mount up over a lifetime, believe me."

"Hmm, OK; I take your point about 'young lady' when you put it in that context. I'd think of that as sounding sleazy from men but a solidarity thing amongst women; so many of us want to be thought of as young, but I hear you. About there being nasty people around too; no, perhaps I wouldn't say that to everyone. I'd just say 'safe home' or something like it. Yes; I see the difference. You're right; I did play into a bit of an unconscious stereotype there. Fair enough; have a lovely night and I hope you have an untroubled journey home."

"Thank you. Honestly, that means a lot. And please do give my best regards to Bo."

Yet to finish the last of her own strong coffee, Bethany watched her cousin gather her belongings with her usual practiced efficiency and head for the door.

"Mim?"

The older woman turned around, a quizzical and fractionally impatient look on her face.

"I'm glad you and Bo have each other; that you found one another."

A controlled smile of tightly reined in emotions, the briefest of nods and the jangling bell over the door sounded her cousin's departure in a quickening rush of October air.

18

Sensory Reading Room

Violet Eve: Perth

"See you in a couple of weeks, Tommy; thanks again for your extra cover this week. You've been a godsend with Ash, Crevan and Dana all having been off for various reasons and Bethany helping out in Stirling."

Magnus smiled gratefully at his part time team member who had earned his days off in lieu. He had received a glowing report from Olivia too about how much Bethany's input had been appreciated and how successful her week had been; it had come as a relief. Not that he didn't trust her to do her job well, but he had been concerned about how tiring it would be for her travelling for five days to work in a different environment, for all she had reassured him that she felt able to stretch herself once in a while on the understanding that any subsequent spike in her fatigue would be accommodated. His fellow manager had in fact relayed to him that there were plans that evening with her Inverbrudock friends; Olivia understood that a sumptuous home cooked curry was involved, and that it was expected to be well worth the additional travel time.

There were two remaining customers in the shop; two women who had come in to make use of the popular sensory reading room, which had a growing reputation of its own thanks to Bethany and Diane's creative ideas and hard work to source locally crafted materials and accessories. The two customers had arrived quarter of an hour earlier; one of them in an anxious state, her companion visibly concerned. Magnus could have sworn he saw tears in her eyes when he gently warned them that it was near to closing time; he had already sent a quick message to his partner Kristian to say that he may be slightly later getting home. He locked the door behind Tommy, checked around the shop floor and went to the sensory room to alert the women that they were now alone in a closed building but that if they were comfortable with it, he would point out the CCTV cameras for their peace of mind and keep the room open for them for a little while longer. He smoothed down a corner of the poster for Andy's Man Club which he had strategically placed under the camera; he had a theory that struggling men who had experience of being interpreted as suspicious, who were spiralling towards destructive choices or who intended to harm themselves may habitually take notice of where security cameras were in public places. If one man saw his poster and found his way to help in a world which placed so much expectation on male-presenting people to be tough and keep their emotions buried, it would be worth it, for all Magnus would be unlikely ever to hear about it.

"Thank you so much; we both truly appreciate this"; the companion stepped outside into the short corridor to speak quietly with Magnus as the other woman, now much more relaxed in her body language, sat reading on a large floor cushion. The fingers of her left hand stroked a soft green quilted patch on the blanket across her lap, kneading it like a cat doing the flexing of its claws which people tended to call 'making biscuits'. Her right hand turned the pages of an e-reader; her pale lips mouthed along sporadically as her rocking settled to a rhythm which looked soothing rather than frantic. Magnus could not place her age, or decide whether she looked older or younger than her companion; her naturally curled fair hair fell across her face and screened her lowered eyes.

"It's been a bad day", the companion was saying. "The kind we always know will happen every so often, where lots of little things go wrong; none of them significant in themselves, but in quick succession so that there isn't time and space to regroup in between." Her neat dark bob skimmed her collar as she glanced around the door into the room, checking up in an instinctive move so automatic that it suggested a longtime protective relationship. She turned back to Magnus, sadness in her green eyes.

"Sadly, she learned early on in life that she had to cope perfectly or else; like many autistic people of our generation, there wasn't the knowledge and support available to prevent all of her entirely harmless differences and coping mechanisms from being at best discouraged, at worst punished. There certainly weren't places like this!"

"Yes, I am extremely proud of my colleague who came up with the autistic hygge concept for our sensory reading room along with her best friend, and I have both of their ongoing consent to disclose that they are both autistic women in their forties who went through the same kind of thing you are describing. She is working in our Stirling branch this week, but if you're likely to be in this area again, you may well meet her on a future visit."

"Autistic hygge? I love that! Yes, it would be wonderful to meet your colleague; I'd like to thank her, and I know my sister would too. We both live in Falkirk but we come to Perth once a month or so"; she shook her head as she sagged against the wall for a moment. "We enjoy our days out here; it's such a pity about today and I can't begin to tell you how much your kindness in keeping the room open for us has turned our day around. First my sister got a phone call right before I came to pick her up, asking her to rearrange an appointment at short notice. Then someone parked like an absolute plonker next to the one space we could get, so there was hardly enough room to open the car doors to get out; I had to let Mo out first before going into the space and people coming in were beeping their horns because I was in the way, so she's had the underlying anxiety all day about it being the same when we get back to the car and the added complication of it being dark. She's frightened of bumping against anyone else's car in case she sets an alarm off; loud piercing noise plus potential social flashpoint is nightmare territory for Mo. Then the café we usually go to for lunch was closed; only today, the one day we are through here, and the next place we went to had a different system of service so she was embarrassed about getting in people's way as she tried to process it all. The wind got up, which hadn't been forecast, and it was above her sensory tolerance levels for a while so we had to postpone our walk around the South Inch. We sat in Rodney Gardens for a while and someone came up to us who clearly knew Mo from somewhere but she couldn't place who it was and where she knew them from, though the face was familiar. So although it didn't come out in the conversation, she felt awful because she couldn't introduce us, and she was worried about how that looked to whoever this person was. Our parents, in accordance with how things were for them, were hot on manners and social etiquette; poor Mo was living on her nerves more than any of us knew when we were children and she never lost her fear of making faux pas, even when it can't be helped; she didn't fail to bother, or forget, about making introductions. Her brain genuinely couldn't connect the input in the moment to her database of people she knows. Then we went to get some food; we both wanted to get a few things and had a basket each, and her loyalty card wouldn't scan. On top of that, she was trying to concentrate on untangling the handles of her shopping bag which always get crossed over at the wrong moment however meticulously she prepares and then sorting out the heavier things to go in the bottom from the pile being slung into the packing area at her, so she had precious little left over for the bright and breezy 'How Are You Today' ritual. She did say 'Fine' through gritted teeth while focused so she was basically talking into her bag, but as a result of that, the cashier didn't hear it so she got asked again loudly 'Are you *well*?' To which she replied 'This is a food shop, not a doctor's appointment', and she had a point. Yet she felt like a failure because we're all constantly inundated with memes about how we must *always be nice* because you never know what another person is going through. She knows that the woman on the till is probably told to ask that too. Poor Mo relives every telling off she's ever had, because she's never been allowed to have an off day, and sometimes she hasn't meant to sound snappish but her tone of voice comes out differently to how she said it in her head. I said to her that yes, the cashier may be told to make small talk and that may justify the initial 'how are you' but people need to be able to read the room and anyone could have seen that my sister was stressed and concentrating. I'd stood off to the side because she gets more distressed if I intervene. She'd admit herself that there's a bit of internalised ableism in that, but it's more about how terrified she is that if she lets people help she will become too dependent and lose her ability to get by on her own; the break and treat of having someone with her for moral support and to help if it comes to a crisis would be lost if she got to the point where it was a need rather than an option and she couldn't face doing things on her own at all. She wants to get a bit of practice at using the self-service tills; they don't expect small talk. Not yet anyway! But we've tried a couple of times and people come bustling up to us, trying to rush us rather than let her do it in her own time. If only doing everything quickly weren't the Holy Grail! Goodness, what am I like dumping all this on you?"

"Please; it's no problem at all. I'm so glad you caught us before we closed, and that our sensory room has been of benefit to your sister. What a stressful day for her; I'm glad she has your support."

"Thank you. I do what I can; when we were children, I know I was seen as doing better than she was and I took that at face value when I was too young to know any better. She was always being compared to me even though I'm the younger one. I carry a lot of guilt to this day about how I accepted the praise instead of standing up for her."

"But you were a child; you are seeing that past time through your adult eyes now, through the lens of the knowledge you have gained, which it was not your responsibility to have at such a young age. I hope that you can find a way to be as kind to yourself as you are to your sister Mo."

"Well, I remember the first time I began to question my absolute belief in our parents being right in all they did. We were in a café; near the old ABC cinema as it was then. Mo had started to tell the waitress what she wanted and our mum told her off for not making eye contact, then ordered something plainer for her because she hadn't done well enough to deserve a treat. Our parents honestly believed that they were saving her from a second best life by being so strict about her lack of confidence, as they perceived it. None of us knew that they were in fact fighting against the wiring of her brain. Anyway, there was this other little girl at the next table with her parents; Mo remembers very little about it because she was so stressed, but I can still see her, with the neat yellow band in her brown hair. She got really upset about my sister being told off and punished when she was being polite and not doing anything bad. She said something about how alone Mo looked and how unfair it was. Her parents were mortified, shushing her and eventually marching her out. I saw the sadness in her eyes as she looked back and I often wonder if she was autistic too, and how she got on in life; I can imagine she became quite the advocate and ambassador. Oh, she was so raw; so desperate to comfort my sister, a complete stranger! I clearly remember the anger and embarrassment in her parents' voices as they said her name. She was called Bethany."

Magnus stared, his blond eyebrows almost reaching his equally fair Scandinavian hair.

"Well now. Isn't this a serendipitous coincidence that you both came in here today? You are definitely going to want to meet my colleague whose project this sensory reading room is. She dyes her hair dark blue these days, and her name is Bethany Sawyer."

The two stared at one another as the enormity of a child's empathy finding its fulfilment across the decades fell into place. Magnus held out his hand.

"I'm Magnus Hagen, Bethany's manager."

"Darcy Keenan. And although I call her Mo, my sister is Mollie Peterson."

The long-familiar contours of the passenger seat in Darcy's car helped to chase away the last residual aches; Mollie's brain quiet enough now for it also to spark the internal reminder to fasten her seat belt as her sister got in beside her. The space next to theirs had been empty when they got back to the car, so getting in had been mercifully uneventful.

"Wasn't that kind of Magnus the bookshop manager, and my goodness; we've found Bethany! I know you don't remember much about that time, but how do you feel about perhaps meeting her?"

Mollie's thoughts were frozen; not bad stuck, just a solid block of some unknown colour felt rather than seen; a hue corresponding to nothing on the visual spectrum and therefore impossible to put into words. She pulled out her orange laminated card which she used to tell people she was not currently ready to speak.

"No problem; we'll chat about it at home, or another day. There's no hurry, and I am confident that Bethany wouldn't have it any other way."

Mollie relaxed further into the seat, stroking the padded stress ball in her pocket. The car purred gently into motion. She closed her eyes, a smile quietly dawning.

Magnus set the alarms and locked up the shop, amazed by the happy chance meeting. He pulled out his phone to let Kristian know he was about to head for home; Alex, Kristian's other partner, would be there by now and the three planned to have a meal together. Kristian and Alex would start getting it ready once they knew he was on his way. As he went to tap his messaging app icon, a banner alert appeared at the top of the screen:

Maximum level alert: Major aurora expected this evening. Likely to be visible throughout Scotland on camera and to the naked eye.

Well, he had seen that before but been disappointed by no-shows or ill-timed cloud.

He looked up at the infinite sky beyond Perth; starry even in the artificial haze of the city centre lights, humming an electric energy through every mysterious interstitial structure of its deceptive emptiness.

He was fortunate to have seen the alert; had he left work at the usual time he would have started driving before it came out and then his phone would have remained untouched while the three of them had their family time.

Taking a screenshot before tapping to acknowledge and clear the alert, he opened the group chat thread with Kristian and Alex, adding the image.

"On my way. But how would you both feel about a dark sky road trip before starting on dinner?"

19

Northern Lights

Violet Eve: Inverbrudock

Jason loaded the last rinsed plate which Bethany handed him into the dishwasher.

"Cheers, Beth"; he turned to face her, scooping up Luke who had jumped onto the worktop with a raucous miaow. The sleek grey cat nuzzled his head under Jason's chin, purring.

"Do you reckon we'll see the aurora this time? Des and I have seen it faintly a few times, but never a proper vivid display."

"I don't know; I've never seen it and Diane said the same as you. It's certainly worth a walk down to the beach though; it's such a clear night and the app alert was at the highest level."

The two joined Des and Diane, already gathering their coats, back in the living room.

"Hey, did I ever tell you folks about the time I saw a rainbow backwards?"; Bethany's remembered anecdote, as so often happened, came out of nowhere. "That sounded like the start of a joke someone tells to fill an awkward silence at a party, didn't it! I mean, the stilted gatherings some people find so essential, not proper parties like real friends have."

"What on Earth, or over it, is a backwards rainbow?"; Diane's eyes lit up at the visual catnip of anything mysterious involving light and colour phenomena.

"It was when I was in Inverness one time, years ago, and I went for a walk along by the cathedral. I saw this bright rainbow and I knew there was something different about it but I couldn't identify what it was. The part I could see was in between buildings; because there was a lot of cloud higher up covering the top of the arc, it was only when I got to a more open bit that I realised that what I had seen was the secondary bow. The difference I'd picked up on was the colours being reversed! The primary bow was like a neon sign. I stopped in the middle of the street and went 'WOW!' Fortunately it was fairly quiet; a couple of tourists coming towards me did give me a bit of an odd look, but I pointed and then they did exactly the same. Of course they had cameras with them! This was before I ever had a cameraphone. I was glad they didn't miss out on it, though."

"Wasn't it Isaac Newton who had orange and indigo officially included in the rainbow?", mused Diane. "Of course, he reportedly had links to companies involved in the slave trade too; I'd like to think that if he had lived in this era, he would have found that abhorrent. We can never know. I also wonder how he would have felt about the idea some people have now that indigo should be declassified because not everyone can perceive it as a separate band. I was thinking about that when you were talking about it in Stirling after the funeral; when you were saying about bereavement being a similar, mysterious and not always understood zone."

"Yes; sadly people think that way about more than just rainbows. If you can't perceive or empathise with something, it's not real"; Bethany sighed.

"We'd have had some challenging conversations with Newton one way and another, that's for sure", nodded Des. "Imagine what he'd make of smartphones!"

"Hmm, I don't know", laughed Jason as he locked the door. "Mention the next big Apple drop to him and he'd bolt and hide in the shed!"

As they walked towards the beach their mirth subsided into companionable quiet; all four of them contemplated the soaring promise of the cloudless sky.

"Do you think there are other colours we can't see? I mean, besides infrared and ultraviolet? There's a theory that there are 'forbidden' or 'impossible' colours which are combinations of ones we know, but our brains cancel them out because they are a clash of input to the colour receptor cones in our eyes, and they're different from the secondary and tertiary colours we know of. People claim to have seen them under special conditions but of course they can't describe them because the language doesn't exist; there's nothing in our experience to compare them to", said Bethany. "It's the kind of thing I'd love to believe, but then colour perception is entirely subjective anyway. We cannot know that what we see and learn to describe as a particular colour is what other people see. I'm not talking about colour blindness; I mean how those of us who can perceive a particular colour, do. We can agree that something is red, but we can never know that red itself looks the same to us as it does another person. And there aren't any gaps in the visible spectrum where an unknown colour could fit; we know the boundaries of it and where our own range of perception ends. I don't know; my analytical mind says no, but I'd never want to rule it out."

"Which is fair; logical questioning and an open mind is the optimum way of looking for the truth", said Diane thoughtfully. "For all we tie ourselves in knots, it comes down to something so simple."

There were a few people already on the beach with cameras on tripods or phones held aloft. Bethany gasped as she glimpsed a definite band of green at the horizon on a screen attached to a camera they passed; discreetly pointing it out, she squinted out to sea.

"We need to give our eyes time to adjust", reasoned Diane. "And even if we do see a good display, it's only recently that I've come to realise from reading about it quite how much of a disparity there is between what our eyes can see and what the camera does. It's not as straightforward as a watered down version of all the colours either. A lot of it looks white to many people's eyes and some will see more colour than others."

The endless dark of the night sky stretching out over the desolate chill of the North Sea began to take on hints of detail as their eyes adjusted; more stars became visible, the horizon more defined. Bethany tried to be patient; to not strain her eyes but let this elusive form of nature come to her. A pang of emotion tightened her throat as she recalled her father gently guiding her to be still and wait instead of rushing forward when they were watching for timid wild animals and birds on a country outing. Overexcited and overstimulated at being on holiday, she had needed to be told more than once; she resolutely pushed that part of the memory away. An adult now, she no longer had any constructive use for the sadness of the eventual sharp telling off and atmosphere spoiling the day. She quietly looked forward, hoping that wherever her father was now, he bore witness to her applying the learned lesson.

"There's a real sense that this is going to be a good one"; Diane indicated more knots of people arriving, each finding their own place on the vast sweep of the darkened beach. Groups and individuals nodded to one another; a community of small huddles united by purpose and respect for one another's space, both for uncluttered photography and for the emotional experience. "It's such a pity Sharon's working. I think I'll text her anyway; if she can manage to pop outside on her break, she may be able to find a dark enough space to maybe catch something on her phone."

"Yeah, good idea; she'll want to be able to let guests know too."

"Good point. I wonder if Charlene and Brandon and Ethan will get to see anything where they are." The trio were away for the weekend as part of the gradual acclimatisation for Brandon as he got used to having a third person around his core routines more often.

"Of course; I'd forgotten they were away. Where is it they've gone?"

"Now, Charlene did tell me their itinerary, but I've lost track of it with being on a course all week and travelling every day. They'll be in Fort William now, I think. That's terrible isn't it, being so vague! Being a train enthusiast myself, I should have perfect recall of not only where they've gone but the entirety of the rail timetables involved."

"It's like you say, though; you've been commuting daily and that will have taken up all your mental energy. That and getting the maximum benefit from your course. Obviously we're both on an end of the week high right now because of getting together and now the added bonus of an auroral display, but we both know we're going to need extra downtime; more than a good night's sleep or a chilled weekend. We're neurodivergent, Di. We cannot get around our limited energy. This whole 'should have perfect knowledge and memory at all times of everything to do with our one Special Interest or else we're faking our autism' bullshit is an absolute fallacy, and a dangerous one. It increases our pressure from ourselves and others. Yes, we will remember or notice details when others wouldn't, but we will also forget and miss things when we don't have enough space for them once we've accommodated all we need to hold in our brains in the moment. And when that gets used against us in an area which feels like our true home; like somewhere we finally get to be the ones who know best, that hurts. It undermines us from all directions and detracts from our precious, limited sense of community and belonging. We are made to feel that we've betrayed something we love by not having an unattainable degree of recall, because people have seen a couple of films with extreme stereotypical examples. But we haven't, and we need to reframe where our attachments fit in our fluctuating capacity to sort out what information we need most at any time and how to make sure we take in and keep that. Attachment is no barrier to misremembering, however much we feel we should have the home field advantage and how that advantage should work."

"Yes, that all makes sense. You're right; it's a specific vulnerability which I hadn't thought about quite like that. I don't need to know off the top of my head exactly where Charlene and the lads are and when; everyone is reachable now if needed. Same with the timetables; I know where to find that information if I need it. Whereas I did need that extra headspace this week to take in everything from my course. It's a bit like supernumerary arcs in the rainbow, come to think of it; the pinks, purples and greens you occasionally see inside the primary bow. They form when the raindrops are fairly small and of a consistent size; it's lovely to see them but the rainbow isn't inferior if they're not there. They come from the light source interacting with the inside of the drops and teasing out more detail; more nuanced combinations of the main colours. When the water coming into the path of the light source is more erratic and inconsistent, that extra detailed processing doesn't happen. In the same way, when the input we need to process is less straightforward, what we can retain is distilled to the main end to end order with no scope for add-ons. I'm glad we've been talking so much about rainbows; I genuinely hadn't thought of it that way before but I will find this helpful going forward."

"Me too. That's the kind of analogy I need for explaining things to myself as well as other people; free from value judgements and ableist priorities. I'll always ask this despite knowing the likely answer; is it OK for me to quote your theory to other people?"

"Of course it is, and I do appreciate you asking. It's been quite a week for you too; you had your own daily commute, and an unexpected need to meet Miriam! How did that go, if you want to talk about it that is?"

"It went surprisingly well"; Bethany described the gist of the conversation.

"That's progress then; well done all round. It's good that she was honest and had the integrity to face you properly. I hope she keeps up her new inclination to listen and be accommodating."

"I think she will. At least, without presuming anything, I feel I can give her the benefit of the doubt. Even though I did get told off in advance for looking as though I were about to 'get myself worked up'. I wish I could learn how to stop my facial expressions getting me into trouble! But how can I when a lot of the time I don't know what they are? It's like working in a cinema where I'm expected to know what's showing on the screens but somebody else is in charge of that technology; I'm tucked away in a booth so I can't see that the display has changed and it may or may not be compatible with the schedule of films I have in front of me!"

"See, now it's my turn to reframe expectations! If Miriam is sincere about learning from your lived experience, that's the kind of thing she needs to take on board. And so well expressed; the cinema comparison makes your point vividly."

"Thank you, and yes; fair comment. I'm not quick enough to think of these analogies at the time I need them though, and it's not always appropriate to communicate them afterwards. I mean, I think I could now to Miriam, especially if she did that again; snapping at me for the wrong look flitting across my face. I need to raise it with her about referring to my mum's house as my 'home' too; for instance, at the wake she was talking about me 'moving back home'. She accepts *that*'s not going to happen, but referring to it as 'home' is still problematic. It's erasing the reality and worth of the adult life I have built as a householder in my own right; it annoys me when people do that to any single person because it's more work, cost and responsibility for a sole occupant, no matter whether the property is rented or owned, yet folk don't respect that it counts as the person's home because they don't have a partner. It implies that they're merely 'playing house'. I'm biding my time on that one though; picking my battles, because I do want to curate a more positive relationship with my cousin and her wife. However, if you take someone like Ginty"; Bethany shuddered; "Virginia Flett, across the road from Mum. That's a whole different story."

"Yes, Des mentioned her appalling behaviour when he gave you a lift home that time. I was furious and wanted to check in with you, but didn't want to bring it up unless you did; I knew you might well have filed it away and not want to relive it."

"Yeah, apparently I 'Looked Put Out' when she said she couldn't take me into town with Dad's burial clothes. What the hell does that even mean? Sure, I was anxious. It was another adjustment on top of an errand which was stressful in itself. That doesn't mean I blamed her, or begrudged her any plans that prevented her from being free. And I didn't say anything wrong. What I could control, I did. But I could not catch whatever '*look*' it was in time. I can't believe I earned a rebuke for that. Autistic or not, who attacks a bereaved person for a facial expression?"

"Precisely. You did not 'earn' that reaction from her. Is it something you feel you need to resolve?"

"Oddly enough, now I think about it, no. I'm still uncomfortable with anyone being displeased with me, but Ginty Flett is simply not important to me. Yes, she's a friend and neighbour of my mother, but she's nothing to me. I'm coming to realise that I need to get better at letting some of these injustices go for the sake of my mental resources."

"You already are getting better at it. I can see it; you possibly can't right now, but trust me, it is happening."

"I feel like I haven't started to grieve properly for my dad though; that I should be more sad, crying more; I don't know, *feeling* more. I feel detached a lot of the time. Is that an autistic thing, do you think?"

"It's a grief thing. Nobody has to grieve to a timetable. Yes, I do believe that autistic people often grieve differently; I know people who have been surprised by their responses to different bereavements and felt that they didn't conform to the expected hierarchy. People who cried for weeks when a friend died but have never cried about family members, and I don't mean because of estrangement. I think a lot has to do with how our brains have subconsciously prepared us."

"Yes, you're probably right. I know to expect the unexpected; that it will be something I'm not prepared for, something outwardly trivial that eventually sneaks in under the radar and sets me off. It could be tomorrow or years from now. I expect that's the same for a lot of people, whatever their neurotype."

"Definitely. None of us can know how we're going to feel until we're in that situation. There is no right or wrong way to grieve; worrying about that is a superfluous drain on your resources."

"I had to let go of the expectation of being prepared for everything I would feel. When Mum had her cancer scare, I changed their house number from 'Mum and Dad Home' to 'Parents Home' in my contacts, so that I wouldn't have to delete one or the other when the time came, but it still didn't look right once Dad was gone so I eventually changed it to 'Mum Home'; perhaps 'Family Home' would have been better than 'Parents'. I couldn't project, at the time, my cognitive understanding far enough to get how it would feel. I don't think anyone can. I thought I'd prepared enough by anticipating that it would upset me whenever I caught myself saying something about my parents and had to amend it to the one remaining. That hasn't touched me, though it has happened quite a lot. I'm grateful for the detachment when it keeps me functioning with apparent dignity in front of people but then I worry about what will catch me out, and at the same time, about looking cold!"

"You've done so well, and prepared as much as anyone could. That was a sensible idea about changing the name in your phone, but nobody can or should expect anyone to predict how their emotions will run their course, however well organised they are. Which you are, much as I know it doesn't feel that way to you."

A burst of exclamations around the two women drew their attention back to the sky as Des and Jason looked around to check on them. The horizon had a distinct glow now; milky white to Bethany's eyes, but as her gaze panned upwards, the flickering she saw had a growing shimmer of green. It was so elusive as to catch her peripheral vision more fully than her direct gaze, but once seen, it infused the unfolding spectacle with a colour diverging from white; subtle as the apple-white tinge of the second floor landing she remembered so well from her exploration of her Aunt Carole's house that long ago Christmas Day. She raised her phone and opened the camera, squealing in amazement as the rich emerald folds shot with momentary high-up shafts of garnet revealed themselves.

"My God! This is the real thing. It's like the universe is flapping and stimming!"

She took photo after photo, her mind reaching to comprehend this gift of a hidden spectrum which she was seeing and not seeing. The starry canvas of the night sky took on a three-dimensional, complementary structure as the lights danced in and out of arcane celestial rooms and passages. The rays and curtains could have been flexing among the portals and hiding places of a cat tree, or sweeping and billowing throughout a towering mansion with multiple split levels, half-landings and twisting stairways. After who knew how many minutes, two more familiar voices filtered through from somewhere behind her on the beach.

"Sharon! And Paulie; oh, I'm so glad you both managed to get here to see this!"

Bethany hugged her cousin and then Sharon's partner. Paulie's eyes were wide with awe; they too had waited a long time to see a display like this.

"I can't stay more than five minutes or so", Sharon was saying; "I have to get back to the hotel, but hey, to see this for even a moment!"

The six of them stood side by side, looking out and up; their phones picking up what their eyes could not as the aurora continued to play across the sky. One set of input and experience flowing into another; a complex of fleeting patterns whose true scale could only be appreciated by the combined scope of watchers and the equipment that supplemented their natural perception. A chain of unique and defining moments flared out from beyond known visibility, binding vigilant lives together in a circle of light on the cusp of the seen and the unseen.

20

Nexus

Perth Station

Bethany looked out to sea as the train picked up speed down the East Coast towards Arbroath, its first calling point on her way home. The carriage lights reflected across a sky which still held the energy of the auroral display; she wondered how many of her fellow passengers had any idea of the show which had been going on far above their heads.

Her hands itched to open up her phone's photo library and begin sorting through the images she had captured, looking for the best ones to save and to share. With an effort of will she waited for her M-ticket to be checked; it would frustrate her if she got started and then lost her place because she needed to come out of the app to bring her ticket up on the screen. Nervous energy fizzed through her; she fought the urge to tap her feet on the floor and drum her fingers on the tabletop.

"Tickets from Inverbrudock, please; anyone joining at Inverbrudock." Bethany was relieved that the voice sounded female; despite being in a good place, she did not want a dose of Tristan overload to disturb the equilibrium. In fact, wait a minute; better still, was that Alison's voice?

"Hi, Bethany!"; well, blessed be, it was. "I haven't seen you for a while; how are you bearing up?"

"I'm getting there. In fact, I've just seen the Northern Lights properly for the first time in my life!"

"Really? Come to think of it, I did hear something on the news earlier about a good display being expected tonight. I'd have gone to take a look if I'd been off today; I should have been, but for some reason Tristan didn't get an email about a shift swap and he had already made plans so I agreed to work. Did you go to the beach in Inverbrudock?"

"I did, with a few of my friends; my cousin and her partner managed along for a quick visit too. I took rather a lot of photos; they'll take some sorting through!"

"Ah well, I'd better scan your ticket so that you can get on with that! I'm so glad you've been able to have such a lovely experience after the tough time you've had this year." Alison pointed her scanner at Bethany's phone and it read her ticket with a validating 'beep'. "Now, I did hear that there's a survey coming out and the link will be shared on the train operating companies' social media feeds. I believe they are going to be giving details in the associated blurb about the passenger user groups and how to get involved, so if you're interested then I'd recommend you keep an eye on our feed for that."

"Yes; I'm absolutely interested, thank you! I will look out for that. It would be easy to miss it among all the posts by passengers saying how much they enjoy staff being extra cheery and having 'witty banter'. I can't begrudge anyone their enjoyment, but it makes my blood run cold knowing the sort of thing they're talking about and how badly I cope. In fact I wonder if part of what some of them mean by enjoying it is that they find it entertaining seeing the likes of me come unstuck."

"I honestly don't think it's that, but I understand why you feel that way and it is valid. Most people, though, genuinely are focused on themselves and getting through their own day, with whatever trials and tribulations it may hold. I'm not saying that to trivialise how you feel, I promise."

"No, I get it, and it's reassuring. I hate feeling like a circus exhibit and as you know, I resent being made to feel like one when all I'm doing is getting from A to B. The lack of choice in being put in that position."

"Of course, and it is something we need to consider; where those boundaries should be."

"I did have a card to display with my Railcard saying 'please be patient; I may need a little extra time to process', but that tended to change how people interacted with me. They would do The Service User Voice; slow and loud, often leaning right into my personal space. I'd be waiting to get off, other passengers around me and they would come up and do it again, especially coming in at Platform 7 at Perth because of it being low and a bigger step down from the train. The other people waiting to get off would be staring at me wondering why I was being yelled at for being a klutz! I eventually stopped carrying the card after one guard started reading it out loud."

"Goodness me, that should never have happened."

"I know. He wasn't being flippant; he stopped and apologised once he realised what it was, but he'd read enough to give the people sitting nearby the general gist. Those cards are such a good idea, but they need a less ableist environment so that people can use them with peace of mind and expect to be treated with the same respect as any other passenger. By which I mean being discreet, respecting their privacy, not writing them off as completely useless, and talking to them in an age-appropriate way; it's perfectly possible to slow down without being loud or leaning into people. When people like me stop using these kind of things, or don't want to wear a lanyard, there's more to it than internalised ableism. Though I'm the first to admit to having my share of that. It's not a simple matter of wounded pride. The success and personally safe use of these devices, which are valuable in themselves, depends upon how people react to them in terms of making them a barrier when they ought to be helpful to both sides and break down barriers."

"Absolutely. I truly appreciate your take on all this, and your willingness to speak out. You enjoy organising your photos, and keep a look out for that survey link."

"I will, and thank you again. It means so much to be listened to and believed; to have my concerns acknowledged as real even when your perspective is different."

Alison moved on through the train, calling for any more Inverbrudock tickets. Bethany smiled at her narrow escape as she returned to her phone. How fortuitous was that; Tristan not getting that email? She was indisputably too tired to stand up to the social neurological overload from him, and today was not a day to be torn down by that. Opening her photo library, she scrolled to the last picture before the start of the multitude she had taken tonight in order to begin sorting those. The copy she had scanned of the image from over a century ago; kept with her on her phone while most day to day photos were saved to her computer and deleted from the device to free up memory, filled her screen as she tapped on it. Newborn Harriet's eyes shone out from a technology undreamed of in her lifetime; holding an enduring quest to connect in their alert, seeking gaze.

Bethany nodded, smiling back.

The aurora images would certainly keep her busy until Perth. She deleted a few immediately as being too blurry, not straight or duplicates; one or two which did not have a flat horizon but which she wanted to keep for their content escaped the delete button because she would allow herself to use the phone's sliding scale 'straighten' feature if she wanted to keep an image and nothing else was wrong with it. Eventually she had whittled it down to thirty images, which she duly posted. She would wait until she got home before deciding which ones to use with the app that made postcards out of her photos; she would send a couple to her mother, one to Aunt Sylvia and Uncle Ray; to her friend Elaine in Inverness and to a couple of people who had been penpals in their younger days, with whom she still exchanged Christmas and birthday cards. In fact, yes; she would send one to Bo and Miriam too. She smiled to herself as she made a mental note to add their address to the app. Small steps; a gesture, a caring check-in, an open mind and she would see how it evolved. She didn't expect or aspire to them becoming close, but they could be friends.

"We will shortly be arriving at Perth."

Bethany gathered her belongings, checking them at least as many times as the automated announcements advised. The loved, familiar platforms flowed alongside the train; the long ramps and soaring pillars in graceful elevation, the modern glass waiting shelters holding a stillness in awe of their surroundings. She stood at the door, waiting for the conspiratorial blink of the 'Open' button once the train had come to a polite halt.

The cold air was a sensory shock after the warmth of the carriage, but in an enlivening way even at this time of night after a long and eventful day. Bethany checked meticulously for the gap between the train and the curved platform; thankful for there being no-one around to startle her, break her concentration and disrupt her centre of gravity by shouting a warning from offstage. Yes, that would be another one for the survey; why did people do that when someone was clearly concentrating, then get offended when it was pointed out that such a distraction at a key moment was dangerous?

Safely off the train, she took a deep breath and counselled herself to relax. Yes, she was beginning to feel overtiredness creeping in, but she had done everything right. She nodded towards the blurred figure of Alison as the train departed, not wanting to wave and distract *her* at the safety critical stage of the train leaving the station. She walked slowly as was her habit; she loved how the moments of quiet descended in the wake of departing trains and would swear to anyone who would listen that she could sense each new layer of journeys made as it drifted, uniformly unique as snow, to settle into the latticework of memories this place gathered.

Up the stairs from Platform 1 to the covered walkway which crossed the Aberdeen to Glasgow line before it converged to the south of the station with the line from Inverness. How much more complex the network had been when this place was built! The thought of that past, bustling time played out in sepia tones in her mind's eye, matching the brown and cream around her as she crossed the walkway, her very present-day footsteps softened by the non-slip flooring.

Down the steps at the other side and around to the tunnel leading to the admittedly stark, utilitarian clash of the small concourse with its ticket gates, locked open at this time of night in the era of getting by on economical levels of staffing. Its cold dark blue and flecked white reminded her of the enamel scrape of some picnic ware which she remembered from childhood; a harsher feel but nonetheless part of the thrill of travelling.

A glance past the concourse towards the end of the tunnel, which emerged into the true heart of the station; the lingering grandeur of Platforms 3 and 4 and beyond, at the start of the Highland Main Line.

Mississippi Mud Pie! The thought came to her in a sensory echo as she recalled her musings on what desserts the colours of the station reminded her of when setting out on her fraught journey to Cambusmenzie. Caramel cheesecake was one of them, but she knew there was something else not so everyday that the deeper shades of the oldest parts of the station called to mind. That was it. A thoroughly lush dessert too.

She began to turn towards the ticket gates, her contented smile matching the gentle peace of the station at that small internal mystery being solved...

Hold on a minute. What was *that*?

Sure, she was tired. Extremely so. But that didn't generally make her hallucinate. She was sure that she had seen a small dark-coloured cat stroll past the end of the tunnel; certain enough to go and investigate.

Bethany hurried towards Platform 3; a strange, liminal place, almost disused except for sidings traffic whereas Platform 4 was the usual for southbound services and the northbound ones used the distant Platform 7, past the two bay platforms used for local services to and from Edinburgh. She looked up and down the long, wide expanse which ended at sidings to the north and the confluence with the Aberdeen platform to the south.

Could she have imagined it after all? It had been a long day, and tiring, albeit a happy and positive fatigue.

A movement caught her eye, up on the footbridge to the north of the main one; overshadowed in its entirety by the towering roof and by lacking the ramps and through route to the other platforms and exit which kept its southern neighbour firmly in the limelight. The lonely structure was mainly used by staff and occasionally by passengers who got off trains further up Platform 4 and crossed the first bridge they came to, or were avoiding the crowds heading for the main one.

Yes; there it was; a petite shadow moving behind the latticework of that footbridge towards Platform 4. Conscious of not wanting to attract negative attention, Bethany headed for the steps of the main bridge and crossed, hoping to intercept the cat over there and prove to herself that she was not seeing figments of her imagination. She got ready to explain if any staff appeared and challenged her; prepared to pretend that she had thought the cat may be limping and wanted to check on its welfare.

It was sitting next to the surprisingly broad steps of the old footbridge. As Bethany approached and held out her hand to it, the cat stood and walked towards her, its paws making no sound at all. She stroked jet-black fur so soft it gave the impression that the warm body beneath was not wholly there; that it was solid but in another time. For a brief instant, the cat looked up at her; tail twitching at the tip in friendly feline endorsement, a silent miaow of greeting as it blinked serene eyes before turning to resume its dignified walk along the platform.

Those eyes. Surely not. It couldn't be?

It had to be a trick of the light. That, or the stories of the past which she had heard at Charlene's, or a combination of both. That had to be the logical explanation, but she could almost have testified in court that this cat had one blue eye and the other was golden yellow.

She stared as the cat stalked off towards the shadows; its tail quivering like a memory of steam.

Vivien always said he had gone on somewhere else; that he was travelling onwards as a true railway spirit, turning up wherever he was meant to be.

The hairs on the back of Bethany's neck and along her arms stood up. She blinked several times, looking around to ensure she was alone before hesitantly calling out.

"Obsidian? Sid?"

It was no surprise to Bethany that there was no longer any sign of the cat on the empty platform. Needing something solid to centre herself, she closed her fingers around the handrail of the steps. The impassive pale padparadscha-toned glare of the station's modern lighting on the rails of the Inverness line seemed to soften into something more natural; somewhere further north and much longer ago.

The Master of Strathruan Station raised a glass of single malt whisky as he paused at the window of his cottage which overlooked the tidy platforms. For that single, private sliver of time, the setting sun caught the top of the rails and turned them to a vibrant colour which reminded him of red-gold hair.

In that instant, Bethany's consciousness overlapped with that of Dùghall Strachan as he silently acknowledged a loss; he stood with the pain, trusting that it would pass. Knowing that these moments honoured a part of him which had its time, but took nothing away from the happy equilibrium of his life here. It was a life he would not change for anything. He smiled as Vivien walked into the room; seeing something in his eyes which told her all she needed to know, his sister slipped her hand into the crook of his arm, rested her head against his shoulder for a moment and stood quietly beside him, wordlessly tapping her own glass against his. The siblings watched and drank their whisky as the sunset faded, before seamlessly resuming their preparations for a prompt start to another day on their tranquil branch of the growing railway. On an armchair by the fireside, a little black cat stirred and awoke contentedly purring.

Time and the light shifted and cooled once more. Bethany stood on the platform, looking at the stretch of steel which had always drawn her mind to imagine adventures in a kinder place. Her own long-held secrets now in generations of context, she felt a dawning of that kinder place within herself.

She slowly uncurled her grip on the handrail of the sedately inclined steps which would always evoke a gentler age. "Thank you", she whispered, before turning back towards the main footbridge; her calm and measured footsteps absorbed into the station's sentient hush as she moved forward into the violet hue of her own time.

Afterword: Dealing With Bereavement

Every bereavement is unique. I have tried to incorporate, through the progress of this story, a general guide to the immediate stages as well as various key pieces of advice and guidance through other characters' interactions with Bethany and Sheila. I will summarise some key points here for easy reference. This guide is not exhaustive or definitive.

For UK readers outside Scotland, please be aware that some terminology and processes are different under the Scottish legal system, though the basics are much the same. When I went through my second loss of a parent, less than a year after the first, there were already subtle differences; what was done via a telephone call the first time was an online process the second time. Technology and working practice changes are inevitably going to generate some of these variations; a difference, however small, can feel extra disorientating especially if you are coping with an additional bereavement before having fully processed previous loss, and there is no timetable on that.

The key is to remember that you are never alone. There is always help available; from people whose job it is to get you through whichever stage of the administration is relevant to them, and although it is new to you, they are used to the practical steps. Most companies such as banks and utility providers have leaflets giving guidance, including advice on taking care of your own wellbeing and signposting you to various sources of help.

There are things you can do to prepare, or to help someone else prepare if you anticipate them having to be at the forefront of dealing with your own passing:

Know any relevant employer's policy on bereavement leave.

Make sure that there is a valid, up to date will, especially if the intended beneficiaries are not granted automatic legal succession rights.

Have a list of important assets (things like: property; vehicles; valuable jewellery, antiques and other collectables; money, stocks and shares) and an estimate of how much they are worth.

Appoint a professional executor if you can, especially if your estate will be substantial (for instance with a property to sell).

Keep all important documents, such as birth and marriage certificates, insurance, proof of ownership of valuables, details of pensions and benefits, GP details, in one secure place. Ensure that the people who will need to access it know where it is.

Make sure wishes regarding type of funeral, burial or cremation, organ donation etc and any pre-existing funeral plans or preferred funeral directors are known; it takes a lot of anguish away from loved ones if they can know for certain that they are carrying out the deceased's wishes. It can be a difficult conversation to have and a lot of people feel that it is morbid or somehow tempting fate; it can be helpful to prepare a sheet of paper with a heading like "Funeral wishes" and leave it for the person to write down things like music, prayers or readings in their own time in private. If you are the one making the notes, ensure that if you want a particular version of a piece of music (for instance recorded at a specific concert or with a particular guest musician), that it is detailed in the notes. Even if your loved ones are familiar with it, you will be surprised at how much can slip people's minds in the unavoidable stress of processing a loss and having to get on with the immediate arrangements. If you are the one making the arrangements and there are gaps in what you would like to have known of your loved one's wishes, be assured that you can only do your best; take quiet time to invite memories to come back to you; ask other people who were close to your loved one. If there is not a funeral plan in place or a known wish for a particular funeral director to be used, choose one which feels right and safe to you; they will help and advise you regardless of whether there was any preceding contact made.

If you are likely to end up responsible for or staying for a time in a property, including your childhood home, which you have never been in charge of: ensure you know the practical things you may have taken for granted. Where all instruction manuals, keys, meters, fuse boxes, water shut-offs etc are located; the codes for any alarms; how to work heating systems, timers etc; what needs to be switched off or left on; where notes are kept for anything which is not automatic or prompted such as booking a central heating service. However much time you have spent living in and visiting a familiar home, there are things which you will not know if you have not done them before. My parents lived in the same house all of my life; I still got caught out by not having a key to one of the locks on the back gate, purely because I had never seen it used. My father always locked up at night and after my mother died, he was the one to open the gate in the morning. I always respected the psychological importance of that to him and left it well alone; whenever visiting as an adult, I would only be coming and going when the gate was propped open. I simply never observed him doing it; as there was a manual bolt on the inside of the gate, I never thought of the actual lock. I made sure I had a set of keys to the house and knew where they were; answered yes in good faith when asked if I had house keys and tested them since they had not been used for a long time, but failed to double check that I *knew of and had keys for every lock in use*. As a result, when I arrived at a time my father was in hospital, I did not have all the keys I needed to get in; fortunately the neighbour who had spare keys was home. More thought and detailed preparation on my part while things were still going relatively well with my parents would have spared me a lot of stress, embarrassment and added damage to my self-belief at a time when my neurodivergent coping skills were already being tested to their limit.

If a death is expected and you are going to be the one breaking the news to family and friends, you might find it helpful to check with people in advance how they would prefer to be contacted when the time comes. A typed message can feel unduly harsh; a phone call, especially to a mobile, could be received in a busy or noisy place. (If the person who is dying does not want others to know their prognosis, then you will need to respect that.)

When someone dies, there will be sensory changes to the body in which they lived; nothing can fully prepare you for these changes when it is someone very close to you, but knowing what to expect can blunt that shock. I was fortunate in that both my parents died in hospital and I was spared the trauma of finding them, checking for a pulse and calling a doctor. The sensory experience was nonetheless deeply unsettling. The body of your loved one, especially if elderly or at the end of a terminal illness, will be likely to look shrunken; something more than asleep. Their skin may look sallow and much paler than it did in life; it will feel cold in a different way from when a living person is cold; stiff or limp depending on how much time has passed, and possibly have a waxy texture. There can be sounds and movements soon after death as air and electrical impulses run down. It is a transition unlike any other; it is still them, yet it is not them any longer. You are on the cusp of their physical presence being handed over to the memories you have of them; it is vital to allow yourself space for this momentous change. (This relates to natural death. Tragically there are circumstances where damage has been done and loved ones see sights which nobody should have to cope with. I cannot claim to know how that might feel, but once again there is trained help available and you do not have to cope alone.)

Everyone feels differently about whether or not they want to see their deceased loved one when they have been prepared by the funeral directors and are in a chapel of rest. It is OK not to; some people find it helpful and comforting but others prefer to remember the person as they were in life. There is no right and wrong; the same applies to visiting a grave or site where ashes were scattered. A memory box may be more helpful. It is a deeply personal choice and nobody should be pressured.

If you are going to be scattering ashes, you may find it helpful to see images of what cremation ashes look like before you have to see those of your loved one. You can search online, or ask your funeral director for advice. Ashes typically weigh around 4-6 lb or 2-3 kg. It is very important to find out whether you need permission to scatter them at the chosen site; the local council can help you with this. Make sure you scatter where any wind will blow ashes away from you and other people.

Everything will feel strange, including what is familiar and unchanged; you may be running on adrenalin or you may hit a wall of fatigue. There are things which need to be done as soon as possible; letting other family members and close people know, registering the death and getting in touch with a funeral director. These are the most immediate tasks and the step by step guides in the Links section have more information, about those and what needs to be done after that in terms of informing banks, utilities, TV licensing, the DVLA (for vehicle owners), Government departments for pensions, benefits and tax, their local council for council tax and travel concession cards, landlords or mortgage providers, insurance, mailing lists, memberships and subscriptions. The Tell Us Once service covers a lot, but not all, of the Government and council related offices; the guidance you receive with the link to it from the registrar will tell you more. If the person who has died was the sole householder and owned their home, you will need to consider whether to close the property down as soon as possible or whether you will need to continue using it yourself for a time, depending on your own needs and how far you have to travel.

Order several copies of the death certificate if you can afford it; each counts as an original, which you will need more than once, and it is more difficult and complicated to obtain extra copies at a later date.

It is important to take care of yourself financially. Banks can release money from the account of the person who has died in order to pay for certain costs such as a funeral, flowers and a headstone. If there is not enough money, there are bereavement specific grants and loans available; the Citizens' Advice Bureau or local welfare rights office can help you with this. If an organisation such as the Macmillan service has been involved, they have a wealth of useful contacts and advice too. Utility bills for the person's home, if nobody is going to be continuing or taking over living there, are paid for out of the estate; any debts are also part of the estate. If you do pay any bills or debts, make sure you keep a receipt and make it available to the executors if applicable. It is important to seek financial advice promptly in the event of difficulties arising, rather than ending up in debt.

If you are in the situation of needing to clear a house to be sold, this too will feel overwhelming. There are clearance firms who will do this for you; if there is a professional executor in place, they may be able to arrange this as part of their service. They will be obliged to keep beneficiaries informed and check all quotes with them for approval. You and any other family members will need time to ensure that you have taken everything from the house that belongs to you or has sentimental value. If doing this bit by bit, keep a note of all you have taken or put out of sight, and what still needs to be removed. There is nothing which you can expect to be guaranteed to remember; your mind may well deceive you. I learned that lesson the hard way too; after my mother died, I did not take her wedding ring, out of respect for my father while he was alive. I put it away, telling him where it was, so that he could find it if he wished but not be upset by coming across it unexpectedly. After he died, I was convinced that I had already taken the ring home and realised too late when I was looking through other jewellery at home, by which time it had gone with the house clearance. Even when my parents' neighbour asked me about a jewellery box (not where the ring had been kept), it did not jog my memory. I now have to live with that, and I confess it here to show that I am not claiming to have done things so well myself nor to have all the answers, as well as to demonstrate that a usually meticulous approach and self-imposed high standards are no match for the stress of times like this. Please, for your peace of mind and in honour of my organised and fiercely perfectionist mother, write things down however obvious you feel they are at the time.

I have already said this, but it's worth saying again: There is no timetable on grieving. From my own experience, the best advice I can give is to expect the unexpected. It is unlikely to be from an obvious cause, or at an expected time, when emotions hit you. It will be something outwardly trivial that sneaks under the radar and catches you. For autistic people in particular, both our actual emotions and how they show in our expressions, reactions and communications can be different from what we and others expect. We can seem detached or we can find that the most random, inappropriate things spark a much needed laugh. You may never grieve in the manner you or others expect. There is no set rule about how soon or how much you will cry; you are not 'behind' or 'stuck' because you have not shed, or wanted to shed, some predetermined quantity of tears. You need to get to know yourself all over again in many ways in order to track your own wellness. The pressure to fit in with conventional expectations is one burden you can, and must, set aside for your own safety. Checking in with your trusted people is more important than ever while you reset yourself.

You may be disproportionately affected by not knowing why, particularly if a death is unexpected or happens sooner than predicted. Talking it through is vital; one conversation may not be enough. Taking it in and processing will take as long as they need to. Bereavement counselling can help if you feel overwhelmed; there is often a waiting list and a requirement for a minimum amount of time (often six months) to have passed since the person died. This relates to organised, ongoing sessions with the same person; helplines are available at any stage.

Your executive functioning (being organised, planning and completing tasks) can take a major hit. You can and will forget or overlook things which will shock and distress you when you realise. This may well be worsened by losing track of your own important self-care such as regular meals and sleeping, because of the stress and because you are thrown out of your regular and familiar routines in so many senses. It is a double shift; the loss of the person and the loss of their part in your routine, and it is exhausting at a time with so much to do that cannot be put off. The people around you can play an important role in helping and gently encouraging you to maintain as much of a schedule of hydration, eating, sleeping (and equally important time awake but resting quietly), fresh air and gentle exercise as you can. Bethany and Sharon make the important points that when menopause is added into the mix, people really are up against their own minds and bodies, and that this will apply to many people at the time of dealing with parent loss.

As Bethany finds herself forced to justify when confronted by Ginty and by Miriam, bereavement is a sudden, drastic change which opens up a bigger gulf than usual between what is expected and required of your life skills and how effectively you can function. You have fewer of your own resources available right when some of those around you often expect you to be stepping up a gear; setting your neurodivergence aside as though it were an add-on which can no longer be "indulged". Self-help guidelines don't usually include this word, but… BULLSHIT.

I hope that everyone who sees this and needs to hear the message can hold on to this fact: **you cannot become**

neurotypical or non-disabled to suit other people or situations, however urgent and valid the needs involved.

It does **not** mean that you are selfish or don't care.
It is **not** disrespect for or betrayal of the person who has died.
Having and honestly declaring limitations and boundaries is **not** "making it about you".
It is **not** new or an invention of the Internet generations; at the same time, you are **not** responsible for the people like you who were born in less enlightened (but in other ways, less pressured) times without access to the knowledge or vocabulary to describe their struggles. Some of those people may be, or may have influenced, the ones putting pressure on you. Have compassion, but own your responsibility to guard your own health.

You are not alone; you need and deserve support. Your worst moments are more relatable than you think. Bethany's awful taxi experience is based on a real incident in my bereavement journey, though I embellished aspects of it in order to show the process of how and why such things can happen. Bereavement is raw; like Sheila says, it's messy, and you're not going to get everything right. It hurts; that matters. You matter.

Solidarity, and a gentle virtual hug if you wish,

Katherine.

Author's Notes

This is a work of fiction. All characters including the author Morton Pargeter, the TV sitcom "Trials" and the comedy heist film watched by Bethany and Sheila, the towns of Inverbrudock, Cambusmenzie and Strathruan, and the Baronet Heights area of London are all my own inventions. The wording of the aurora alert on Magnus' phone is not a direct representation of any real app. The rail travel and bereavement related staff with whom Bethany interacts, her workplace and her colleagues do not represent real individuals or companies. Autism Initiatives' one stop shops and manager Matt are real, used fictitiously with kind permission. The featured businesses in Stirling are real, with the exception of Murray Dunsmuir's law firm.

Although Murray is fictitious, the practical guidance he gives to Bethany is all applicable in Scotland and the UK. It is based on my own experience and research; although lived experience absolutely counts, the advice in this book should not be taken as a substitute for legal or professional input.

I set out to write this book after my mother died; my father's age and health at that time meant that he was not expected to outlive her by very long. He died nine months later. I wanted to use my experience of that turbulent time to help other autistic people in similar situations; to bring some structure and an idea of what to expect. Although this is primarily a story about the autistic adult experience of bereavement, my ongoing themes around aspec (aromantic and asexual) and other LGBTQIAP+ belonging and representation are strongly continued in this book for two main reasons. One: to show how the pressure of being in multiple marginalised groups can add to and interact with bereavement stress as well as magnifying other types of loss which are bereavements in themselves; two: because wider understanding and belonging of minority identities are achieved when representation is included where people are not directly looking for it. Similar types of incident occur more than once for much the same reason; to convey the exhausting cumulative effect and the importance of solidarity, knowing others have been there too.

Special mentions to Ann-Marie, Chris and the team at Co-Op Funeral Care who helped me with making arrangements, and to my probate case manager Ethan at Co-Op Legal Services who has empathised and been a rock throughout a long and complicated process.

Thanks to Penny, Loryn, Mark, Stuart, and all at the Royal Highland Hotel (Inverness), Radisson Blu Station Hotel (Perth) and Golden Lion Hotel (Stirling) who welcomed and cheered me on as I stayed in their accommodation on bereavement related travels and writing breaks.

Railway family shoutouts:
Appreciation to Nicole King for seeking out the term "anemoia" (answer provided by Brian C Johnson) and posting so evocatively about it in a railway context.
Thanks to the staff at Perth Station for goodwill to all train enthusiasts and for not batting an eyelid at my interest in their workplace and questions about that old footbridge!

Thanks, love and light to all three Autism Initiatives one stop shop teams in Scotland, to David and Gwen Morrison at PublishNation UK, and to my own support network without whom I would not have been able to get this far: Ann, Bridget, Gabi, Ian, Jeni, Karen Catalina, Karen Kaz, Kathleen, Kathy, Keelan, Liz, Lizzy, Lynsey, Matthew, Sarah and Tam.

Sources and further help

Support and guidance: Procedures and terminology

UK Government bereavement advice:

https://www.gov.uk/when-someone-dies

Scottish Government bereavement advice:

https://www.gov.scot/publications/death-scotland-practical-advice-times-bereavement-revised-11th-edition-2016-9781786522726/pages/5/

Coroner and Procurator Fiscal:

https://www.odt.nhs.uk/odt-structures-and-standards/organ-donation-retrieval-and-transplantation-teams/role-of-hm-coroner-procurator-fiscal/

Emotional support

CRUSE Bereavement Support:

https://www.cruse.org.uk

Samaritans (UK):

Call 116 123 (free; does not appear on your phone bill) or email jo@samaritans.org

Crisis support by text message (UK):

Text SHOUT to 85258

Other useful links: Autism

Autism Initiatives Scotland one stop shops

Highland:

Highland One Stop Shop (highlandoss.org.uk)

Tayside:

Perth One Stop Shop (perthoss.org.uk)

Edinburgh, Lothians and Borders:

https://www.number6.org.uk

Autistic led and run advocacy organisations

Autism Rights Group Highland:

ARGH – Autism Rights Group Highland (arghighland.co.uk)

Scottish Ethnic Minority Autistics:

https://sema.scot

Scottish Women's Autism Network: non-binary inclusive:

https://swanscotland.org

Amase (Autistic Mutual Aid Society Edinburgh):

https://amase.org.uk

Autistic / neurodivergent authors and books

Kala Allen Omeiza:

https://kalaomeiza.com

Elle McNicoll:

https://ellemcnicoll.com

Chloé Hayden:

https://www.chloehayden.com.au

Katherine May:

https://katherine-may.co.uk

Black, Brilliant and Dyslexic (edited by Marcia Brissett-Bailey):

Black, Brilliant and Dyslexic | Jessica Kingsley Publishers - UK (jkp.com)

Neurodiversity consultancy with neurodivergent members

The Autism Network (Scotland: includes Lynsey Stewart, she / her):

https://theautismnetwork.co.uk and https://www.l-mac.co.uk

Marion McLaughlin (they / them):

https://www.auroraconsulting.scot

Aromanticism and asexuality

AUREA:

https://www.aromanticism.org

AVEN:

https://www.asexuality.org

Cora Ruskin (author):

https://corastillwrites.wordpress.com

Evelyn Fenn (author):

https://evelynfenn.co.uk

Madeline Dyer Statham (writes as Madeline Dyer / Elin Dyer / Elin Annalise; strong intersectional disability representation):

https://madelinedyer.co.uk

Sounds Fake But Okay (Sarah Costello and Kayla Kaszyca):

Sounds Fake But Okay Podcast (soundsfakepod.com)

Eris Young (transgender author; identifies as queer):

https://erisyoung.com

Yasmin Benoit (Black asexual activist):

https://www.yasminbenoit.co.uk

Sources and interest

Thin slice judgements (Terra Vance, neuroclastic.com; original source Noah J Sasson et al, National Institutes of Health, 2017 "Neurotypical peers are less willing to interact with those with autism based on thin slice judgements"):

Free PDF download: Thin Slice Judgements and The Different World Autistics Inhabit » NeuroClastic

Allosexual and alloromantic: experiencing a 'typical' amount of attraction; pan, bi, homo or hetero. For allonormative / amatonormative meanings and distinction: "Amatonormativity: What is it and is it harmful?" (Suzanne Degges-White, 2023):

What Is Amatonormativity? (choosingtherapy.com)

Campaign Against Living Miserably (CALM):

https://www.thecalmzone.net

Andy's Man Club:

https://andysmanclub.co.uk

Pareidolia:

Neuroscience: why do we see faces in everyday objects? - BBC Future

"Forbidden" or "impossible" colours:

https://www.londonvisionclinic.com/these-are-the-colours-your-eyes-cant-see/

Isaac Newton:

Colours in the rainbow

What are the colours of the rainbow? - Met Office

Reported links to the slave trade

Isaac Newton's London life - Big Issue North

Inclusion of cyan in the colours of the rainbow:

Colors of the Rainbow (scienceinfo.com)

Supernumerary arcs in the rainbow:

Supernumerary bows - Cloud Appreciation Society

Glasgow's Finnieston Cranes:

How A Disused Crane Became The Symbol Of Glasgow - Sangwin Group

Heterochromia (two different coloured eyes) in cats:

Understanding Cats with Different Colored Eyes - Cat Tree UK

Queen Victoria and rail travel:

History of the Royal Train - The Story Behind the Royal Family's Train (townandcountrymag.com)

The Faroe Islands "Diamond Sound":

https://www.heraldscotland.com/news/18770944.faroe-islands-200-miles-scotland-another-world/

Aurora Borealis spotting (Glendale Aurora app):

https://aurora-alerts.uk/

That grand apartment building in Stirling where Bethany imagines it would be fabulous to stay: You can, and it is! Parts of this book were written and edited and its title was chosen while staying there:

https://www.oldspittalhospitalapartment.com

About the Author

Katherine Stirling Perthshine Highland (she / her): an autistic and aspec author living in Scotland.

Using my own experiences to promote understanding, inclusion and belonging is my mission in life. That includes putting some of my worst moments out there, albeit fictionalised. I wrote a book of coping strategies guides and a compilation of autism positives balanced by realism before moving on to fiction with my Inverbrudock trilogy. I enjoy using autistic joy, a dash of humour (often irreverent), a sprinkling of profanity and a hint of the paranormal alongside the eternal battle against ableism in my fiction, and there is always at least one cat.

Proceeds from my writing go to support the work of Autism Initiatives in Scotland, whose one stop shops have been a mainstay in my life for many years. Alongside my own time of bereavement, I wrote this book during a poignant coming to terms with the end of an era in my own life. After twelve years in the Highlands I plan to relocate to Perth, where that station I love will become my local base and calm silver light gently illuminate the rest of the seasons of my life.

A note of tribute and respect to my parents, who never knew about my writing as some parts would have distressed them. They did their best with no support raising a struggling child who nobody then knew enough to realise was neurodivergent. (My author name is a pseudonym.)

You can find my books in Kindle and paperback format on Amazon, or contact any of the three one stop shops.

katherine.highland@pnwriter.org

Printed in Great Britain
by Amazon